Gringos and other stories

Michael Rumaker

Gringos and other stories

Grove Press, Inc.
New York

Contents

To: Sy Lowenstein
   Rosalynde Singerman
   Cornelius Walters

Exit 3

The tractor-and-trailer rolled slowly off the shoulder and onto the turnpike, its red and yellow lights blinking. Jim stood a minute watching it go, then leaned down and picked up his suitcase and started walking briskly along the exit road, past the brightly lighted toll booths. He walked faster, tucking his scarf tightly about his throat as a cold wind sprang up. The exit road made a sweeping curve downward, joining the main highway a hundred yards on. He shifted his suitcase to the other hand and headed toward the highway.

As he walked along a Chevrolet convertible pulled up beside him, the motor idling. The horn blew. Jim turned, staring blindly into the headlights, and kept on going. The horn blew again, the car inching alongside him. The window on the driver's side rolled down and a head poked out.

"Hey, buddy. C'mere."

Jim hesitated a moment, then stopped and swung around, staring past the headlights and squinting his eyes to see better. He saw a sailor's white cap.

"C'mere a sec', buddy."

"Whatta you want?"

"C'mere, c'mere," the sailor persisted.

"I'm in a hurry," said Jim, swinging his suitcase to the other hand.

"It'll only take a minute."

9

Jim walked over to the car, stooping down and peering at several dark shapes in the back seat.

"Whatta you want?"

"Little favor," said the sailor, turning and smiling up at him, his arm slung loosely over the wheel. "Just a weensy favor," he grinned, crooking his thumb and forefinger small.

There was a commotion in the back seat. Two of the dark shapes were wrestling with a third. The third was shouting and swearing at the other two.

"Lemme alone! Ouch, you bastards! I don' wanna go!"

"G'wan, get outa here," snarled one of the dark shapes. "You're pissy-eyed."

"C'mon, soldier, this is where you check out," snapped the other. "Exit 3, soldier."

"Don't call me no soldier, goddamn it, don't you call me no soldier!"

"So, okay, marine boy. Hop to it. Here's harbor, baby."

"Just don't soldier me, goddamn it. Just watch what you call me."

"Now's that the way to treat a buddy?"

"Okay, buddy, okay, babydoll."

"You see," grinned the sailor, reaching out and taking Jim by the arm. "He's a little looped."

"So what's that got to do with me?"

"Now look, mate," said the sailor. "He lives around here somewhere, see? Gotta get a bus to get home'n see his folks. You know."

"Look, sailor, I don't want the responsibility," Jim said, backing away. "I plan on getting home myself sometime tonight."

The sailor clutched his arm firmly. "Take him off our hands, will you? We're sick of him. He's been driving us nuts all the way up from Carolina. Come on, be a pal."

"You better take him to a bus stop yourself."

"Buddy, we don't know nothing about this burg. We're heading for Boston."

The two were struggling with the drunken marine, trying to push him out of the car on the other side.

"I don't wanta go!" shouted the marine. "Lemme alone! Damn you, stop shoving me!"

"Out you go, Pluto." They each gave a violent shove and the marine flew out of the car, hitting the asphalt on his backside and folding up in a heap. He sat there stunned, his head swinging from side to side.

"Hey, don't think you're gonna dump him on me!" Jim shouted.

"Toss out his bag," said the sailor.

"Alley-oop!" A leather suitcase was pitched out the back window and landed in the grass off the shoulder of the road.

"Get this crate rolling!"

"Boston, here we come!"

"Hey! Wait a minute!"

"Thanks, matie!" the sailor called, stepping on the gas. "You're an angel, baby!"

The car leaped forward, shooting around the wide curve bending out to the highway, the tires screaming.

Jim threw down his suitcase. He plonked his hands on his hips and spat furiously over his shoulder, as the tail lights of the convertible disappeared in the traffic. He glared over at the dark heap a little distance away. It was swaying back and forth on the road.

"Who the hell are you?" he said, taking a step toward him.

"Buddies . . . yeah . . . some buddies . . ." came a voice out of the dark heap. Jim kicked his suitcase onto the shoulder and advanced toward the marine. The marine was moaning to himself, buried in the folds of his raincoat.

"Come on." Jim leaned down and grabbed him under the arms. "Before you get run over."

"Let 'em run me over."

"Can you stand up?" Jim slapped him on the cheek.

"You're goddamned right, buddy. I'm a fucking american marine, remember that."

"Okay, stand up." Jim stepped back, watching him. The marine's head popped out of the collar of his raincoat and jerked from side to side. He looked up blearily at Jim in the darkness.

"You a doggie?" he said thickly.

"Get yourself up off the pavement."

"I'm a fucking american marine," he growled. "I can take the cold."

"Come on, get up." He reached down and grabbed him under the arms. "You gotta walk, don't you?"

"I can walk."

Jim strained and grunted as he pulled him up. He managed to get the marine on his feet, then clasped both arms around his middle, supporting him.

"Can you stand alone?" he said.

"I'm a fucking marine, I tell you."

"I know, I know. Can you stand alone?"

"I can stand alone."

Jim released his hold and took him by the arm. The marine swayed back and forth, his heavy boots scraping into the cinders as he struggled to get his footing.

"I'll never forget this, buddy. You're a peach, real peach."

He reached around, lifting his hand to touch Jim's cheek. The hand was crudely wrapped in a dirty handkerchief damp with blood. His knees buckled and he grinned, his eyes rolling loosely in his head, as he placed the hand on Jim's shoulder.

"What'd you do?" Jim said, trying to push the hand away.

"Window!" laughed the marine, his head flopping on his chest. "Doggie. Only he was on'a other side'a window . . . smashed . . ." His head flew back and he shouted, "Smashed the fucking doggie!"

"Hey, cut that out. Look at yourself."

"I'm a slob. I don't give a shit."

"You can't go out on the street like this. Tuck in your shirt tail, fix your tie."

"Okay, buddy, you're pretty swell, buddy."

He began fumbling with the front ends of his shirt with his one good hand. The shirt was streaked with vomit down the front. He gave up trying to stuff the shirtends into his trousers, and the bad hand moved up, clawing dumbly over his tie, smearing it with blood.

"I can't do it, buddy," he said, letting his hands fall heavily at his sides.

Jim squinted his eyes, then spit over his shoulder.

"Why them guys had to dump you on me I don't know."

He took the shirtends and pushed them down inside the trousers. He had soiled his hands from the vomit and he took out his handkerchief and wiped them, muttering to himself. Then he straightened the marine's tie and squared his cap straight on his head, pushing the mop of oily black hair under the

stiff crown. He pulled the coat together and buttoned it.

"I'll never forget this, baby, I never will, honest."
He tried to put his arm around Jim.

"Okay, okay. Just stand still."

The belt of the raincoat was twisted in back. Jim
straightened it out, evening the lengths, then
buckled it tightly in front. He held the marine at
arm's length and looked him up and down.

"You're okay, buddy," said the marine, raising his
hand and wiping his nose on the bloody handkerchief. "You're okay." He tried to touch Jim, but
Jim pushed the hand away.

"You puked all over your tie."

"In Virginia it was. Vomited all over Virginia."

Jim pulled the lapels of the coat together and
buttoned them, hiding the tie.

"We're going down there," he said, pointing to
the highway. "See?"

"Okay, babydoll. Anything you say. Anything."
The marine leaned over suddenly and kissed Jim
clumsily on the mouth.

"I thought you were a marine," Jim said, looking
around for the suitcases.

"I'm a red white and blue marine, fucking american marine, true blue."

"Can you carry your bag?"

"I'm not helpless."

Jim steadied him, then walked over into the grass
and picked up the leather suitcase belonging to the
marine. When he got back he found him squatting
on the asphalt.

"Whatta you trying to do?" He thrust the bag at
him. "Let's get outa here. It's colder'n hell."

"Damned col'," muttered the marine.

Jim pulled him to his feet, slipping his arm into his and grasping it firmly. "Take this." He handed the marine his suitcase.

"Okay, baby. Anything. Anything you say."

Jim picked up his own suitcase and they started walking arm-in-arm, the marine stumbling clumsily, bumping at his side, down the exit road toward the highway.

"Tell me where you live."

"Nowhere." The marine tried to spit, but the saliva plopped on the shoulder of his coat and dribbled down the sleeve.

"Tell me where you live so I can put you on the right bus."

"My old man's gonna meet me exit 3."

"This is exit 3." Jim looked down toward the highway. "I don't see no car waiting."

"Call . . ."

"Call what?"

The marine stopped, pressing a hand to his forehead.

"Call . . . 2477 . . ."

"That your phone number?"

"Yeah."

Jim said the number to himself a couple of times.

"You're sure that's right?"

"I wouldn't kid you, baby."

"We'll find a telephone. I'll call him. How'd he know what time you'd get here?"

"He knows. Right now. Mr. Stark, my father, you ask for him. He knows me. Tell him I'm home. . . ."

The marine dropped his suitcase and fell on his knees, clutching his stomach.

"What's the matter with you?" Jim cried, bending down beside him. "You feel sick?"

The marine was crying.

"Hey," Jim said, shaking his arm. "You gonna vomit? Make it snappy."

The marine didn't say anything.

"Come on, get the hell up outa there. We gotta get moving." He pulled him by the shoulders, but he wouldn't budge. He swayed back and forth, weeping.

"I smashed his face," he moaned. "Cut it all up. I showed him. Cut his face to ribbons. Ground his face in the broken glass. He won't make faces anymore. I ground his pretty face to bits."

"Quit talking like that. You'll get locked up."

"Let them lock me up. I fought in it. I know what it's all about."

A car came along the exit road, slowed down as it passed the two men, then stopped. A window slid down and a man's voice called, "Hey, soldier, can I give you a lift? Always glad to help our boys. Can only take one. How 'bout it, soldier?"

The marine straightened up slowly, then sprang forward and cupping his hands to his mouth shouted, "You go stick that ride! You gook, I know you." He started running for the car, stumbling and sliding over the asphalt. Jim started after him.

"Gook! Gook! Kill 'em!"

"I don't take no drunk," the man snarled. "Soldier or no." He stepped on the gas and the car tore off, gathering speed as it raced toward the highway.

"You keep your junky car, you goddamned gook!" shouted the marine, standing in the middle of the road and shaking his fist at the retreating automobile. "I know you. Know everything about you!"

He leaned forward, folding his arms over his chest and rocking back and forth, began to weep again.

"Whatta you wanta do that for?" Jim said, hurrying up to him. "Guy wants to give you a ride and you act like that. Come on, here's your suitcase. Let's get to a telephone."

"Let him stick his car."

"Look, I'm getting pretty sick of you."

"Okay. Okay, babydoll. You're okay. You're a real buddy." He put his arm around Jim's shoulder.

"Will you do like I say?"

"Sure, baby, sure."

"You start acting funny again, I'm gonna leave you here cold and flat."

"Don't do that, buddy," the marine said, squeezing him tightly. "I'll do what you say, buddy. Honest I will."

"Okay. Grab your bag and come on."

They came down to the highway and walked into the blue light of the tall roadlamps standing at intervals along the way. Turning right they followed a narrow dirt path running alongside the concrete shoulder. The four-lane highway was crowded with traffic moving swiftly in either direction. The marine was having difficulty walking and he leaned heavily on Jim's shoulder.

"You walk too fast," he choked.

Jim slowed down, keeping his eye on the neon signs of some gas stations further up the highway.

"Look," he said, "when we get to one of them stations I want you to behave yourself. You got me? No blabbing about gooks or anything. You understand? Clean up your mouth. People don't like to hear that kinda talk. This isn't the army."

"Goddamn it, I ain't in the army. I ain't no goddamned doggie."

"Okay. You just hold yourself up and talk straight. You hear?"

"I hear you, baby," said the marine, coming to a dead halt under a roadlamp. "I hear you talking all the time."

"Now what?" said Jim, dropping his suitcase.

The marine lifted both hands, holding them close to his face, clenching and unclenching his fists. He winced, staring at the bloody hand as though he hadn't seen it before.

"I did this, buddy. I killed a doggie in Virginia. Killed 'im through a window," he said, slowly uncoiling the sticky fingers. The blood-clotted handkerchief slipped to the ground, was picked up by the wind and carried off in the darkness.

"Now look what you done," Jim said.

The marine sighed and leaned heavily on Jim's shoulder.

"I ain't feeling no pain," he said, gruffly, trying to stuff the hand in his pocket. "It don't hurt me."

"It's damned near cut through to the bone. Here." Jim pulled his handkerchief from his pocket and took the hand.

"Aw, buddy, I don't wanta do that. That's your clean handkerchief."

"It's not so clean." Jim took the hand and wrapped the handkerchief around it to form a crude tourniquet.

"That's mighty white of you, buddy. Mighty white."

"Yeah, now come on. We gotta get moving."

A little further on, in a flat open area on the other side of the highway, stood a glowing telephone booth, red white and blue plastic and glassed in on three sides.

Jim jerked the marine by the arm. They crossed the highway, Jim keeping a tight hold on the marine as they dodged their way through the traffic. When they got to the booth, Jim made the marine sit down on the suitcase.

"Stay put now. What was that number again?"

"What?"

"Your phone number. I wanta call your father."

"I forget."

"Come on, don't get funny."

"Okay, buddy, I wouldn't get funny with you."

"What is it then?"

"Wait a minute . . ." He shut his eyes tight and after a moment said slowly, "2477."

"Okay. Now you just sit here."

"Buddy . . ."

The marine tried to get up.

"Stay there for godssakes."

Jim made him sit down again.

"Buddy . . ."

"What?"

"If he ain't there, try the Columbia Café. That's . . ." He paused a moment, shutting his eyes again. "I know it. A minute. I know it. Yeah . . . 8191. You call there he ain't home, huh, buddy?"

"Okay. Don't move. I'll be out in a minute."

Jim stepped into the booth, pulling the door closed after him. He fumbled in his pocket for some change, found a dime, and dropped it in the slot. He dialed the first number. The phone rang again and again, one long, one short. There was no answer. He swung around to check how the marine was and saw only the leather suitcase overturned outside the booth. He looked quickly around the vacant lot to one side, then spotted him staggering out toward the middle of the highway in the midst of the traffic. The hand wrapped in the handkerchief was lifted, a bent cigaret hung loosely between his lips. He was pointing to the cigaret and motioning to a Negro sailor who stood on the opposite side of the highway, thumbing a ride. Jim flew out of the booth and ran over to the edge of the highway.

"Hey, get back here!" he shouted.

"Buddy, you got a match? Yo, dinge!" the marine was calling in a slurred voice over the roar of the traffic. "Yo, buddy-dinge," he howled. He lurched toward the Negro, pointing to the cigaret.

"Hey, sailor!" Jim shouted.

The Negro was waving his arms, motioning the marine back.

There was a screech of brakes as the car bore down on him. The driver swerved to one side, narrowly missing him. He slowed down long enough to shout out a few curses, then sped on.

"Hey, sailor, stop that guy, will you?" Jim started across the highway. "He's drunk!"

The Negro lifted his bag and dodging a tractor-and-trailer, ran out to meet the marine. Both Jim and the Negro got to the marine at the same time and each took an arm and led him back across the highway.

"Wanta match," said the marine, as soon as they got to the telephone booth.

"I gotta match. Whyn't you ask me?"

"You was busy."

"You coulda got killed."

"Yeah, man, you shouldn't go bumming lights on a busy street the shape you're in." The Negro pulled a lighter from the pocket of his peajacket and cupped the flame, holding it out to the marine.

"Much obliged, buddy," he said, puffing hard on the cigaret. He swung away and slumped against the booth. "Mighty fine, dinge, mighty fine of you."

"Look, sailor, you stay here a minute and keep an eye on him, will you? I'm trying to call his folks."

"I wanta get to New York before midnight," said the sailor.

"This'll only take a minute, pal. Honest."

"Hey, dinge, come on over here and talk to me," growled the marine. "Pretty nice for a boogie. Saved my life. Give the dinge the purple ticker."

"Don't you call me that."

"Lay off that stuff," Jim said to the marine. "He saved your life. He gave you a light, didn't he?"

"A spade's a spade. He's a good old spade." The marine slid down the booth and slumped in a sitting position at the base of it.

"Look, will you stay here a minute?" Jim said, taking the sailor by the arm.

"Boy, I told you I wanta get to New York. I ain't got no time to mess around."

"Just a minute, huh?"

The Negro glanced down at the marine, who sat propped against the plate-glass wall of the booth, his face buried in the lapels of his raincoat.

"Well, okay," he said slowly. "But I don't mean to stay around here much longer. I probably missed a dozen rides by now. You hurry up and make that call."

"That's swell of you," Jim said. He stepped into the booth, sliding the door to after him. He dialed the number of the Columbia Café and there was a long wait as the phone buzzed on and off at the other end. He kept glancing down to where the marine sat slouched against the glass, his knees drawn up to his chin. The Negro stood off a little, his hands thrust deep in his pockets, his collar turned up. He was looking down the highway in the direction of New York, watching the cars speed by.

Finally the receiver clicked at the other end, there was a hum of voices and the straggly tail-end of a blues being sung in a drunken, wavering voice.

"Hello, hello, Columbia Café?"

A shrill giggle hurt his ear.

"That's right, kiddo. Whadda you want?"

It was a woman's voice.

"Is Mr. Stark there? I gotta talk to Mr. Stark right away."

"Who?"

"Stark—Mr. Stark—His son—"

"How do you spell that, kiddo?"

"S-t-a-r-k, I guess."

"You *guess*? What you want him for? Hey, Harry, make mine VO with soda, if you're buying!"

"Listen, is he there?"

"Who?"

"Mr. Stark."

"Say, what's your name?"

"What's that got to do with it? All I wanta know is if Mr. Stark's there. I gotta talk to him about something important. His son . . ."

"Geez, I sure wisht they had television on phones. You got an awful cute voice."

"Look . . ."

There was a rapping at the door of the booth. Jim glanced up and saw the Negro motioning toward his watch. Jim nodded quickly and held up his finger. "A minute . . . Just one minute."

"Who's that knocking? Who're you talking to, cutie? Ouch, Harry, don't get so fresh! Hello . . ."

"Look, this is awful urgent. Could you please get me Mr. Stark. His son is drunk . . ."

"His son? Who's his son? I don't know his son. What's *your* name?"

"Look, that don't matter. I gotta talk to Mr. Stark 'cause his son's laying outside here stone drunk and I want Mr. Stark to come and pick him up."

"What's wrong with being stony drunk, I'd like to know? You should be happy. Whatta you say me and you get stony drunk, huh?" She tittered. "Where do you live?"

"Look, lady, all I want is a little simple information. Now don't get funny with me . . ."

"Who's getting funny? I like that."

"Is Mr. Stark there?"

"Who?"

"Oh, goddamn it to hell!"

"Look, kiddo, don't think you can use that kind of language with me, just 'cause I can't see you. I ain't truck."

The Negro started rapping on the door again.

"Just a minute! Just a minute, please!"

The Negro shook his head firmly and picking up his canvas bag started walking quickly toward the highway.

"Look, lady!" Jim blurted in the mouthpiece.

"You're hurting my ear! And quit calling me 'lady'."

"I'm sorry. For the last time, is Mr. Stark there?"

"Who's that you're talking to?"

"Nobody."

"You talk to yourself?"

"Look, once and for all, is Mr. Stark there?"

"No, he ain't here."

"Jesus H. Christ!"

"Where're you calling from, kiddo? Whyn't you and your friend come on over? Hey, Harry, put my drink there . . . Hey, kiddo . . . Hello . . ."

Jim slammed down the receiver and shoving

open the door, got up and jumped outside. He stood over the marine, hands on hips, scowling. He looked up and down the highway. The Negro was nowhere in sight. He leaned down and slapped the marine hard on top of the head.

"Wha . . .? Wha . . .?"

"Come on, you. Get up. We're getting out of here."

He pulled the marine to his feet.

"Wha . . . Wha'sa matter?"

"Come on. We're gonna find a taxi station. I'm gonna put you in a cab and goodbye, baby. You're getting to be a real pain in the neck."

"Okay, buddy, anything," mumbled the marine. He yawned loudly and stared around stupidly with sleepy eyes, leaning on Jim. "Anything you say . . ."

Jim handed him his suitcase and flung one arm around him and they started walking toward a cluster of neon signs ahead.

"I couldn't get your folks."

"My folks?"

"Yeah, there wasn't any Mr. Stark at the Columbia Café."

"He must be somewhere else," the marine said thickly, as he stumbled along trying to keep up with Jim. "May be at the Silver Star."

"Well, I'm not going into that again. I had enough trouble making that call as it was. I'm putting you in a taxi and sending you home."

"Okay, baby. I'll never forget this. Honest."

They crossed tree-lined streets, the trees slender and bare in winter, and on either side, stretching down the blocks, low bungalows with warm yellow lights glowing in the windows.

"Pretty. Awful pretty," croaked the marine,

swinging his head from left to right. "Ain't it pretty, buddy?"

"Huh?"

"The lights . . . awful pretty."

"I don't see no taxi station," Jim said, looking around. "I thought there was a taxi station along here."

They walked on. In the next block they came to a drugstore facing on a sidestreet off the highway. The front of the store was one sheer wall of plate-glass window, adorned with flickering neon signs. Inside the cold white light of the place Jim spotted a row of telephone booths. A woman wearing steel-rimmed glasses stood behind a chrome counter, reading a newspaper. The store was empty.

"Look, I can get the number of a taxi from here," Jim said. He hesitated a moment. "Now look, you stay out here. Sit down on your suitcase and behave yourself. You understand me?"

"Sure, buddy, sure, I understand you."

Jim let go the marine to take his suitcase from him and the marine fell back, bumping his full weight against the window. The woman inside glanced up sharply from her newspaper.

"Be careful," Jim said. "You don't wanta bust this thing. That lady's watching us."

"I'll bust it. Bust any window I see," growled the marine. "Bust the doggie."

"Pipe down," Jim said, looking quickly around. "People might hear you. Cop or something. . . ."

"Hate the cops."

"For pete's sake, don't start that again."

"Kill every one of the bastards. Grind 'em up."

"You just sit down here and forget all that."

He set the suitcase against the window and

helped the marine to sit down on it. He put his own suitcase beside him.

"Now, keep an eye on this bag while I'm inside. I don't want anybody stealing it."

"Nobody'll steal it, babydoll. I'll kill them."

"Okay. Now you just sit there and be quiet. I'll be back in a minute."

"Where you going, buddy?"

"I'm gonna call a taxi for you."

Jim stared at him.

"Didn't you call my father, buddy? I told you Columbia Café. He's gonna meet me exit 3."

"Look, he wasn't there. I told you already."

"You didn't tell me nothing. You getting funny with me, buddy?"

"I'm not getting funny with you. For christsake, I..."

"Just don't you get funny, that's all. Nobody gets funny with me. I'm a fucking american marine. Remember that. I don't take no shit from nobody. Smashed a window."

His head fell forward. The woman behind the counter had taken off her steel-rimmed glasses and was staring intently at the two outside.

"Look, I'm trying to help you out," Jim said. "I won't do you dirt. Now sit here and be quiet. I'm gonna get you a taxi so you can get home."

"Okay, baby. You're okay, baby." The marine began roughly fondling him. "I can trust you, baby, I know that."

"Well, okay. Just sit here now til I get back."

"Right you are, I got you, babydoll."

Jim straightened up, adjusting his scarf and smoothing his hair with one gloved hand. He glanced a moment at the woman behind the counter, then strode over to the full-length glass door, pushed it open and went inside. He walked straight up to the woman.

"I need a taxi right away. I . . ."

"Auburn 7-0801," she said crisply, her eyes trained on the marine sitting outside, his back against the window.

"Thank you."

He stepped into one of the booths and dialed the number. The phone on the other end buzzed once, there was a click, and a thick voice said, "Hummingbird cab."

"Listen, I want a taxi . . ."

"Where are you?"

"Where am I? I don't know. Wait a minute. I'll find out."

He pushed open the door and called, "Lady, hey, lady, what address is this?"

"Black Horse Pike, Burr Drugs," she said, not looking at him, her eyes still riveted outside the window. "He knows."

"Burr Drugs," Jim said, swinging back to the mouthpiece. "Black Horse . . ."

"I got you. Be there in a couple of minutes."

The phone clicked at the other end. Jim stared at the receiver a moment, then slowly put it back on the hook. As he was stepping out of the booth, there was a shrill scream from the woman at the counter, and turning toward the window Jim saw the marine standing facing them, his face twisted, his eyes bulging from his head, and the bloody hand lifted high over his head, clenched in a fist.

"Stop him! For godssake, stop him!" screamed the woman, her fingers pressed at her temples. "I knew he'd do something! I knew it!"

"Hey, don't do that!" Jim shouted, running for the door. "Hey!"

The marine walloped the window with his fist. The glass shuddered under the impact. He threw back his arm and pounded the window a second time, leaving a smear of blood where his fist struck.

The woman covered her mouth with her hand and hurried out the door after Jim.

"Stop him! What is he nuts?" she cried, once outside.

Jim grabbed hold of the marine and pulled him away from the window.

"What're you trying to do? You said you wouldn't do anything. Look at you!"

"Smash the fucking window! Kill the bastards!" choked the marine, flailing his arms about high in the air. He was panting for breath and trembling, his face flushed red. Jim held him tightly in his arms.

"Are you crazy or something? Drop them arms! Drop them! Now look what you done to your hand. You got it bleeding all over again. Come on now. Calm yourself."

The marine let his arms fall heavily at his sides. He began to cry, his mouth flapping open and shut as he gulped for air; a string of saliva swung from his chin. He pressed his fists into his eyes.

"Smash it!" he gasped. "Smash it all!"

"Settle down," Jim coaxed. "You're getting yourself all worked up over nothing."

"You get him outa here," snapped the woman, polishing her glasses on one corner of her apron. "I'll call the police."

"Don't do that, lady. He's had a little to drink . . ." He lifted his hand awkwardly to her. "You know."

"A little, huh? Why he's drunk as a hoot-owl. Must have the dt's to carry on like that. He busts that window, I'll make plenty trouble for him. And I'll hold you responsible." She snapped the glasses back on her nose. "Look at the mess he made," she said, pointing to the blood stain. "I just had them windows cleaned."

"He won't bust your window, lady."

"Well, you get him away from there and hold on to him. That's not no ordinary cheap glass," she said, rapping the window with her knuckles. "He busts that it'll cost him a pretty penny."

"He won't bust it, lady."

"Well, I'm telling you."

"Okay, lady, goodnight, lady."

"You hold him over by the curb. He comes close to this window again, I'm calling the cops, and I don't mean maybe."

"I got you, lady. Come on, boy. Come over here with me. Do like I say."

The marine would not move, but kept his fists knuckled over his eyes, his body shaking with dry sobs.

"What's he blubbering about? He got the crying-jags?"

"I guess so," said Jim, leading the marine away. "He don't feel so good."

"I should think not, all he's had to drink."

She stared at the marine, pursing her lips and folding her arms beneath her apron. Jim led the marine to the curb and held him there with both arms around him.

"You just better keep an eye on him, I'm telling you," she said, scratching her arms under the apron.

"I will, lady."

She looked quickly up and down the street then

turned and pushing open the glass door went back into the store.

"Now you see what can happen? You see? She coulda had you pinched."

"Don't care," choked the marine.

"You're acting like a baby. Tough guy, huh?"

"Bust her window," he said, rubbing his eyes. "Grind her face in it. Show her."

"Just behave yourself."

"Cut off her tits with the broken glass."

"Stop that."

"Dried up whore. Let me go talk to her," he muttered, struggling to break free.

"You stay right here. Haven't you caused enough trouble? The taxi'll be here in a minute. And, listen, don't you give the cabbie no trouble. You lay back and get some shuteye riding home. Don't you bother the taxi driver."

"I'll kill him, cut off her balls."

"Lean over and strangle him when you're skimming eighty an hour down Black Horse Pike," Jim whispered hoarsely in his face. "Go on and do that. I'm tired of the whole monkeybusiness."

"I'll strangle him."

Three soldiers appeared at the corner, walking arm-in-arm, laughing and talking loudly. They stopped in front of the drugstore and then turned and stared at each other in amazement.

"This here ain't no bar," said one.

"I be damned if I want an ice-cream soda," said another, and he burst out laughing.

"Fi-yoo!" wheezed the third. "All this shoe leather burnt for nothing, and're my dogs in heat!"

They roared with laughter. The marine cocked his head up and glared over at them.

"Hey!" he shouted.

The three soldiers looked over to where Jim and the marine were standing.

"You an MP?" shouted the soldier in the middle, squinting and bending forward, hanging loosely on the arms of the other two.

"Come over here," snarled the marine.

"Who you shouting orders at, duckboy?" said one of the soldiers. "This ain't the army out here, buddy."

"Don't 'buddy' me. I ain't no goddamned soldier," said the marine, working to pry himself loose from Jim's arms. "I'll show you who the hell I am."

"G'wan, you guys, get going," Jim called. "He don't know what he's saying. He's drunk."

"I ain't so goddamned drunk I can't take care of three doggies," snapped the marine, freeing one arm and thrusting Jim aside. He stood with his legs apart, his hands held loosely on his hips, glowering at the soldiers.

"C'mere, doggies."

"Get *him*!" said one of the soldiers.

The three laughed, nudging each other.

"Go on, you guys," Jim said. "He don't know what he's saying."

"No marine scares us."

"Here's one'll make you shit razor blades," said the marine, taking a step forward.

"Come and try it."

Jim came up to the marine and took him by the arm. "Look, that taxi's gonna be here in a minute. You don't wanta make no trouble."

"Who's making trouble? Keep the hell outa my way." He stiff-armed Jim square in the chest and Jim pitched back, landing heavily in the gutter, the wind knocked out of him.

"Nobody kills a fucking american marine."

The woman in the store walked quickly to one of the telephone booths. She stepped inside, pulling the door shut after her.

"Come on, you guys," said one of the soldiers, reeling toward the marine. "Let's make short work of this bird."

The three of them advanced abreast, staggering a little, crouching low, their knees bent, their arms crooked, and hands clenched into fists. The marine scraped his feet into the grass plot, digging in for footing. He stooped low, thrusting his head out, his lips curled in a snarl, the white hard teeth clamped tight together, his eyes glistening, narrowed to slits.

"Come on, you doggie bastards, come to papa, come on, you fucking doggies, to papa."

He swayed his outthrust arms from side to side and crouched lower. One of the soldiers let out an earsplitting rebel yell and the three pounced on the marine, shouting and snarling, kicking him, beating at him with their fists. The marine's one good hand shot up, swiping wildly at the air. There was the hard smack of knuckles on flesh and breathless choked curses. The marine's knees began to buckle, his one hand disappeared in the tangle of swiftly flying arms and legs. The soldiers clung to him and the marine began to topple, lurching from side to side, and, groaning, sank to the ground beneath the weight of the men. He lay moaning. There was the sound of hoarse heavy breathing.

Jim picked up his suitcase and started walking down the dark street, kicking at the tufts of dead grass in the cracks of the pavement.

The woman had come out of the telephone booth and was standing behind the counter, staring at the men.

The soldiers untangled themselves, piling off the marine, and started hopping around from one foot to the other, laughing loudly, and snorting clouds of steam from their mouths.

"That settles the big-mouthed duckboy!" hooted one, panting for breath.

"Big shot marine! Ho, boy!"

They helped brush each other off, then each started setting his clothes right. One poked around in the grass, hunting for their caps.

The marine lay stretched full length on the grass plot, one arm thrust over his chest, the other pinned beneath him. His mouth was half open, a strangling noise came up from the depths of his throat.

"Come on, men. Let's go find that bar," said one.

"Celebrate the victory!" shouted another.

"Fi-yoo! I hope to Christ this ain't a dry town. No-o-o-o Sahara Mary! Yipeeeeee!"

They took arms and walked away, laughing and shouting, each glancing back now and then over his shoulder, booing the prostrate figure of the marine until they rounded the corner and were gone.

At the end of the street Jim stopped beneath a streetlamp, set down his suitcase, and looked back. He could see the marine stretched out a little distance from the drugstore, and beyond that the headlights of the cars hurtling back and forth on the highway. He coughed up some phlegm in his throat, rolling it around on his tongue, then spit it over his shoulder into the gutter. He pulled up the collar of his overcoat and, rubbing his gloved hands together, looked again toward the other end of the street.

The woman in the drugstore came out, carrying

a sponge in one hand and a little tin of water in the other. She glanced sharply at the marine, then turned to the plate-glass window. Dipping the sponge in the water, she began rubbing at the stain of blood on the glass. She rubbed briskly, pausing once to dip the sponge again in the water and wring it out, then polished the glass clean with a corner of her apron. She emptied the tin of water in the alley alongside the building and came back and stood in front of the window, one hand on her hip, giving a careful inspection of the glass. She walked over to one corner and rubbed at it with her sponge, then stepped back a pace to survey what she had done. Satisfied, she turned and stood regarding the marine for a moment. She went to him in quick short steps and bent over him, reaching one hand out from beneath her apron and slapping his cheek again and again. The low wail of a siren sounded somewhere along the highway. The woman snapped up her head and listened, thrusting her hands under her apron and rubbing them briskly. She stared down at the marine a moment, then her eyes darted up and down the street. The approaching siren grew louder. She spotted Jim standing at the corner and her mouth began to move, to shape words, as though she were calling to him. Jim turned his back on her. He began to shiver and took out a pack of cigarets from the pocket of his coat and lit one. He stuck the cigaret between his lips and, picking up his suitcase, stepped off the curb and started over the street at a brisk pace, heading across town.

Gringos

As the young man moved out over the long concrete bridge leading into the town he shifted the bulging knapsack a little on his thin back and trudged on, stooped, setting his splayed feet down in a slow, purposeful way. He was high-shouldered and scrawny-necked, his shoes broken and spattered with dust, the heels run over from long walking. He wore a sunbleached pair of khaki trousers and a faded shirt with the sleeves ripped off up to the armpits. His face was hawk-like, cracked and seamed with grime, yet milky blue eyes peered out of his sharp face. The end of his nose was peeling and burned red from the sun. Dark circles of perspiration soaked the back and front of his shirt.

To the south, beyond a dry, choked plain where some boys were playing baseball, hills, with scraggly patches of dust-laden brush pushing out on their humped slopes, pressed hard and stark against the delicate light blue of the Mexican sky. It was early morning, but already the sun burned down with a fierce, driving heat, pressing everything flat against the earth. On the roadway of the bridge cars and trucks roared back and forth between the border and the town in the distance, the baking asphalt sending up billowing waves of colorless heat.

At the middle of the bridge he stopped and, slipping the pack from his shoulders, rested it against the railing. Taking a rag of a handkerchief from his hip pocket he wiped the sweat from his face and neck as he watched a group of children below, their tattered cotton shorts whipping at their thin brown legs, as they chased a herd of cattle down the arroyo and under the bridge. The children shouted shrilly at the beasts, beating their great sides with branches. Slow and unwieldy in the soft dust, the animals moved clumsily down the dry bed of the river, their heads swinging low and close to the earth, their thin legs thick with mud and flies. Green strings of saliva swung from their muzzles, spattering the dust.

The faces of the children were curiously solemn and monkey-like. The young man hoisted his sack again and continued on across the bridge.

Claylike, the distant town shimmered in the noonday heat, its low tiled and corrugated tin roofs squat, packed close, thinning to isolated shacks and shanties as the town, wheel-like, spread out over the dusty yellow plain. Beyond the town, to the south, was another ridge of low hills, brown and parched, dotted with clusters of the dark brush. The light on the plain was so intense it hurt his eyes and he turned his gaze to the town where the light was broken, as though absorbed, in the close, bunched roofs.

The bridge shook as a jitney, loaded with Mexicans sitting stiffly in the high seats, roared by, heading in the direction of town.

"Cheeklets, meester?" A small brown boy, barefoot, a piece of twine holding up his ragged pants, leaped out from between the girders of the bridge, holding outstretched to the stranger a box filled with penny gum.

The young man swung out at him. "Go on," he shouted. "Go back!"

He shook his fist at him as though he would strike the boy if he came any closer.

The boy ran ahead and, as the stranger came up, poked his head from between the spindles of the bridge, bowing, again offering his box of gum. There was a little girl with him now and she stood a few paces off, shyly fingering the edge of her dress and looking up at the stranger and then at the boy. The boy nodded to her. The girl started walking around in a circle in front of the stranger, one of her legs stiff and lame, a pained expression on her face.

"*Infortunada*," whispered the boy, shaking his head and looking up sadly at the stranger. "My seester."

The man tweaked his nose, pulling off some of the loose skin from the tip of it, reached into his pocket, brought out some change and thrust it in the girl's hand. He went on his way.

"How much? How much?" the boy cried and, turning, the young man saw the two children running off, the girl, straight-legged, in the lead, clutching her fist to her chest, while the brother tried to catch up with her, snatching for her flying hair and shouting, "How much?" At last he caught her by the shoulders and, wheeling her around, grabbed her hand and pried her fingers open. Taking the coins, he looked at them, then thrust them in his pocket and walked off, his sister beating at his back with her fists, crying.

The man snorted and spit over the railing. Below the bridge at an angle ran a rough dirt road lined with shanties, their sagging rusty tin roofs patched with Coca-Cola signs. A few palm trees leaned among the huts, their fronds ragged and sere, heavy with dust. Half-naked children sat in the middle of the road playing with stones, silently piling them on top of one another. The noise of phonographs and radios blared from several of the shanties, a roar of jazz and Mexican love songs in the hot, still air of noon. In the doorways of the houses women sat, heavily made up, artificial flowers in their hair, each busily fanning her breast, each eyeing the stranger leaning on the balustrade of the bridge above. At the far end of the street two American sailors, their arms flung about each other's shoulders, their white uniforms wrinkled and streaked with dust, staggered from one dark doorway to another, hooting in and laughing raucously, being grabbed at by each woman in turn, then staggering on again. A little distance away another sailor lay sprawled flat on his belly in the middle of the road, his cheek resting in a pool of vomit.

One woman, hip leaning against the jamb in a doorway closest to the bridge, smiled up at the stranger and called, "Ey, *americano!*" She waved, laughing. "You want poosy, yes?"

Up and down the street other women leaned from their doors, lifted their skirts to the hip and waved gaily, taking up the call.

"*Americano!* Come on down. Poosy, eh?"

One woman strutted out into the middle of the road and, loosening the front of her dress, placed her hands on her breasts, tossed back her head and, slowly revolving her hips, began singing to the stranger with coy, downswept eyes, beckoning him down. He began to walk away.

"Gringo!" several shouted, running out into the street and throwing their skirts up around their waists. "Gringo, come on!"

But he just gave a tug at his pack, straightening it a little on his back, and kept on walking.

The girl who had sung to him spat in the dust. *"Chinga tu madre!"* she cried, squinting her eyes and baring her teeth. *"Chinga tu madre, americano gringo! Pa-too!"*

The others burst out laughing and began shouting in a chorus, *"Chinga tu madre, gringo!"*

The town began abruptly at the edge of the long bridge, where the main street curved in toward the plaza, the jagged holes in the soft asphalt filled with loose stones. As the man went under the broad arcades, Mexican men, their hands in their pockets, watched him silently as he passed.

Stepping out in the sun at an alley-like street, he saw a young Mexican standing with his arms folded over his chest, a wet cigaret hanging from his mouth, his flesh and hair glistening in the bright light. He was watching two girls picking over fruit in a market stall across the street. The man went up to him and asked him where the hotel was.

The Mexican looked across the street again at the girls who were glancing back at him now, quick and shy, over their shoulders. Abruptly he unzipped his trousers, letting them drop to his knees. Spreading his legs to hold the trousers up loosely at his kneecaps, he carefully and slowly peeled the flaps of his sweat-soaked shirt from his thighs and buttocks, speaking rapidly in Mexican to the stranger as he did this, yet still watching the girls, and jerking his head, for the stranger, toward a squat, lime-painted building at the far end of the plaza. The stranger nodded. The Mexican was smiling broadly now at the pair of girls across the way. Giggling, the girls were bending closer to the fruit as he tucked in his shirtends and zipped his trousers.

The young man went down the street in the di-

rection of the plaza. He stopped under the corrugated tin awning of the hotel, stepped out to the
curb and looked up at the place. He let the knapsack fall to the street and rolled his aching shoulders
a couple of times, then shot his arms out, flexing
them. The heat bore down on the street with an
overpowering weight. As in a dream, there seemed
an absence of color in the intensity of the sun's
glare. The few Mexicans on the street moved, if
they moved at all, slowly, lifting their legs as
through deep water. Most were slumped against
walls of buildings or squatted inert under the metal
arcades of the shops. There was a shrill, impene-
trable silence over everything.

He kicked his knapsack up out of the gutter and
across the sidewalk. A dog, one of the many stray
ones skulking around the streets, its protruding ribs
sharp as knives, padded up to the sack, sniffed at it
and began to lift its hind leg. The young man
clapped his hands loudly (the sound of his hands
was like the sharp crack of a bullet in the quiet
street) and booted the animal in the haunches. The
dog reared and growled, lifting the dark upper lip
of its jaws, exposing thin, razor-like teeth, then
slunk off down the street, the hairs on its back bristling. Close by a few men who had watched the
scene laughed softly. The young man hoisted his
knapsack and entered the dark, cool lobby of the
hotel.

There was a smell of stale air and Lysol. Behind
the desk the clerk was shouting at an extremely
pale, puffy-faced woman in a tight dress. Her black
hair fluffed out in endless high curls about her face.
She spat on the floor and slammed her knuckles on
the desk and screamed back at the clerk. As the

young man approached the desk the clerk swung around and shouted at him, "No rooms! No more rooms!" and, swinging back to the woman, continued to berate her.

The young man's thin lips tightened and he was about to say something, then changed his mind and reached down for his sack, about to go, when he saw across the gloom of the lobby several shadowy women sitting in cane chairs scattered about the room. The eyes in their pale faces watched him with a bright, flinty intentness. At the far side of the lobby was a narrow doorway with wicker swinging doors. It was a small bar in the darkness of which gleamed a pink neon beer sign. Seated on a high stool near the door was a big, flush-faced sailor, his cap pushed back on his head and a thick shock of reddish hair, oily and sweaty, jutting out over his brow. He was grinning at the young man over the top of the swinging doors.

"Hey, come on over here, buddy," he shouted, "and I'll buy you a beer."

The young man hesitated a moment, then picked his way carefully across the dim lobby, past the women. He pushed open the swinging doors, dropped his pack and slid onto a stool next to the sailor.

"Hey, keep, two beers," shouted the sailor to the bartender, then turning to the stranger, said, "This place's like a reg'lar whorehouse. Don't pay no mind to that pissy-eyed clerk, he thinks you're a bum. All they want's the U.S. sucker with his pesos. But don't you worry, I'll fix it up. You stay in my room. Hell, we can split the bed. I don't mind sleeping on springs. I'd even sleep on the floor except for the goddamned cockroaches. The cockroaches down here *fight back,* for chrissakes. Hell, I don't wanta get humped here anyway. Ja' see the pigs crawling around this place? 'Nough ugly gash to make ole peter wrinkle up next to nothin' and never wanta show his pretty head no more."

The bartender had set the beers down and now the sailor snatched up one of the fresh bottles, stuck the neck down his throat and emptied it in three big swallows. Rubbing the back of his hand over his mouth, he winked and smiled and said, "Christ, that's good brew. What's your name?"

"Jim," said the stranger.

"Mine's Harley." The sailor extended a huge beefy hand to the stranger and they shook. "You in?"

Jim looked at the sailor, puzzled. "What?"

"You know—." The sailor lifted his hands wide, then leaned heavily on the bar. "Service."

"Oh. No."

"Ever been in?" The sailor pulled out a mashed pack of cigarets from his jumper and pushed them at Jim.

"Army."

"Tough shit."

The sailor struck a match for their cigarets, then picking up his first beer and guzzling the rest of it, said, "Come on, grab your gear. I'll show you the room."

Jim chug-a-lugged, picked up his knapsack and followed the sailor out of the bar. As they passed the desk in the lobby the clerk raised a hand to them, his little mustache quivering indignantly.

"Don't gimme any lip, chico," said the sailor, striding over to the desk. "Here," he threw a bill on the counter, "shove that in your hole."

The clerk slid the bill across the counter, looked at it, then smiled at the sailor.

"Goddamned spics'd sell their old man's balls if they thought there was a going price for them on the market," muttered the sailor.

The elevator was stopped halfway between the first floor and the basement. A grease-smudged mechanic was sitting on the roof of the cab, straddling a small motor between the cables, and slapping it furiously with a monkey wrench, a disgusted look on his face.

"That thing ain't worked since I been here," said the sailor, jerking his thumb toward the elevator as they started climbing the stairs. "They don't never get near 'nough juice to run it. Looka that ass—that's the way they fix things down here: keep hittin' and hopin'."

As they climbed, down the long dark halls, several doors stood ajar. In one was a woman half-reclining on a bed, painting her fingernails. In another, a woman wearing a hair-net, her hair wound tight in big pink curlers, stood looking out at them. Now and then they caught glimpses of figures in pale slips going from one room to another.

The sailor's room was up under the roof. As he unlocked the door there was a musty, airless odor even though the small window under the eaves was wide open. There was a bureau, its lacquered surface scarred and burned black with cigarets. There was a chair and a narrow bed. The floor was strewn with dirty shorts, T-shirts and socks.

"This is it," said the sailor, waving his arm about the room and kicking a pile of the dirty laundry away into one corner. "This place is mainly a whore's hangout," he added.

"I ain't blind," said Jim.

"It's a lot cheaper than the other places, though —and not much worse. Hope you don't mind the blood and come stains on that mattress. I tried turning it over but it's the same garden of flowers on the other side."

"So long as there ain't no bedbugs," said Jim. He let his knapsack fall to the floor with a loud thump.

"What you carrying in there?" said the sailor, prodding the sack with the toe of his shoe. "Rocks?"

"Shoes. Must have four extra pair. All busted."

"What for?"

"Walking."

"Where you walking to?"

"Don' know. Mexico City, I guess. I'm just walking."

The sailor was looking at him quizzically.

"Look!" Jim burst out, "I ain't no gangster or nothing. I'm walking away from trouble—at home —I always wanted to walk and see things. Now I'm doing it. That's all."

He was breathing quickly and his hands were trembling, the cords in his throat stretched tight.

"Hell, I don't wanta butt into your personal business," said the sailor uneasily, looking down at the floor. "I never thought you was no criminal or nothing." He looked up quickly. "Don't take offense, buddy."

"You don't mind me staying here, do you?"

"I wouldn't ast you in the first place."

"Well, I'm very much obliged." Jim stuck out his hand and the two men shook. Then Jim stalked over to the window and spat a thin, fierce stream out and turned abruptly back to the sailor.

"I been on the road for weeks now and ain't been

drunk nor humped once. One truck driver in Texas gave me a lift—I had a broke blister on my heel and tried to thumb it as much as I could—well, this big bruiser got funny, but I told him I don't go that route and got off at the next town. Sure are a lot'a queers around these days and they are all big fellas."

He suddenly stopped talking, looking embarrassed and turned his face away, like a man who's not used to talking much.

"I know what you mean," sputtered the sailor. "But damn, it ain't *satisfying*, that's what! Hey, you wanta wash up after all your walking? Maybe the water's running."

"Can you smell me?"

"Hell no."

"Then I guess I don't wanna wash!"

"Come on then," said the sailor, thrusting an arm around Jim's shoulder. "Let's us two go out and tie one on. Jesus, it's good to have somebody to talk to down here. Hardly any these bastards can talk American."

They went down into the steaming plaza and stared at the neon lights in the bar fronts. A young man with carefully combed and brilliantly pomaded hair unzippered his trousers and stepping to the curb urinated noisily into the dust of the square, watching the splattering puddle with an expression of deep and dreamy reflection on his handsome face.

"That guy ain't got no shame," said the sailor. "Look at all these ladies around and him doing that. At home we do it back of the barn or turn away from the house, out in the fields."

"They ain't no ladies around here," said Jim. "Come on."

He took the sailor by the elbow and steered him

to a doorway over which hung a sign, EL SOL. Jim pushed open the swinging doors and they went in. The room smelled of antiseptic. The long bar was lit in a stark, white light. Against the walls, in shadow, Mexicans sat at rough, round tables, big hats low over their eyes, talking in low voices. Long paddled wooden fans revolved slowly from the ceiling.

Jim and the sailor walked to the far end of the bar and sat down on wooden stools, each turning his body slightly to look about the room.

The bartender, a fat man with a thick black mustache, got off his perch and came down and leaned his hands on the bar.

"Tequila," Jim said.

The bartender set down two double shots of tequila and a small plate of lemon slices. He slid over the salt shaker.

Jim laid a couple of coins on the bar and the bartender rang it up on the big brass register. The two men sipped their drink and watched as a young Mexican girl stepped out of the shadows into the bright light over the bar. She walked up to them, her hands resting lightly on her thighs.

"Buy me tequila?" she smiled, circling her arms around Jim's neck and leaning the weight of her heavy breasts on his shoulders.

"Why the hell not!" said the sailor and pounding his fist on the bar shouted for the bartender.

The woman slid onto a stool between them, crossing her legs, her hands clasped loosely in her lap. Jim stood up awkwardly, his foot kicking her stool, and leaned his hip against the bar.

The bartender set a bottle down before them and poured fresh drinks. Both Jim and the sailor slapped bills on the counter and the bartender took the sailor's and after making change, reached into his pocket, brought out a small yellow disc and snapped it down in front of the woman. She dropped the disc between her breasts, then ducked her head to one side and spat in the concrete trough down which ran a trickle of stagnant water at the foot of the bar.

"You working the house?" asked the sailor, suddenly scowling.

Her head shot up and she smiled at him brightly. "*No comprendo.*" She placed her hands together at her cheek and leaned her head to one side. "I sleep, I sleep," she said.

"Come on, old man, let's take a leak," said the sailor, grasping Jim's shoulder and pulling him away from the bar.

The toilet was high-ceilinged and dingy. There was a long zinc-lined trough against one wall and along the opposite wall were several concrete urinals the size of grottoes.

As the two men stood at the trough, Harley said, "I'll tell you, buddy—when I was taking a leak on the ship the other night, I look down at this red, ole wrinkled thing and I say to myself, 'Jesus, the things you bin in—what ain't you bin in?' But that ain't no reason to torment it. That babe out there's just a hustler. Sleep, shit. She's just a chit girl. I just wanted you to know that."

A little man appeared at Jim's side, thrusting his tiny face around to smile toothlessly up at him. His cotton trousers and shirt were greasy and hung in loose billows and folds from his small, bony frame. With a grin he stuck an arm up into Jim's face. Half his hand had been amputated and in the crook of the stump pressed against the back of his wrist were pinched fan-wise, for Jim to see, a half-dozen or so pornographic photographs, smudged and dog-eared. Jim stared at them and then at the face of the man whose dark eyes shone with mute glee as he waved the photos closer to Jim's face. Jim turned away, fumbling at his fly, and stepped quickly around the little man who kept dancing and hopping agitatedly about him with his pictures.

"What's the matter, chief?" called the sailor, poking his head around. Jim jerked his thumb at the little Mexican.

"Christ, can't even take a piss," said the sailor, moving toward the little man. "G'wan, get outa here, stump. Whatcha' got there? Jesus, looka this, Jim."

The sailor held up one of the photos, a wide grin creasing his face.

"He's got 'er right on 'er belly." The sailor studied the picture intently for several moments. "Looks like she kinda likes it."

"I know she did," Jim said. "I posed for it."

The sailor dropped his mouth, looked at him in surprise, then burst out laughing. "Git outa here!"

He fished in his pocket for some change, handed it to the Mexican, then, lifting his jumper, tucked the photos in the top of his trousers, next to his skin. "Save these for a rainy day," he said, then giving Jim a hard thump on the back, said, "Come on, let's get the hell outa this clip joint."

They pushed out of the toilet, scooped up their money at the bar and leaving the girl sitting perplexed, her hands plonked angrily on her hips, were once more out on the street.

The dirt street was a gentle slope of a hill crammed with small, metal-awninged shops and cafés. The two men stepped down onto the broad, rough stones forming the sidewalk, looking from left to right into the dark shops. On the porch roof of one a dog trotted back and forth, paused to scratch at a closed shutter, and trotted to and fro again, whimpering. Near the end of the street an old Ford truck was drawn up at the curb. Two men in rubber pants and vests, stained with blood, were carrying sides of meat on their shoulders into a butcher shop. Jim and the sailor stopped and watched, Jim idly leaning his shoulder against the rear of the van and staining his shirt with blood.

As the man lifted a side of beef from the back of the truck, the springs groaned and the truck rose higher on its axles. A dark cloud of flies swarmed around the truck and as one of the men lifted a side of meat, the flies, blackening the stiff, gristly surface, flew off; as it was carried into the shop, the ragged edges flapping, the flies flew back and covered up the meat again.

Harley nudged Jim and they went on, ducking down a side street into a large, sprawling building where the sunlight filtered thinly through the glassed-in roof. It was a vast indoor market with high-backed stalls piled with fruits and dry, shriveled vegetables the color of dust. The voices of the women had a shrill, metallic sound under the roof as they pushed and elbowed each other at the stalls, brown fingers, like mice, slithering over the fruits and vegetables. From every stall hung the long strips of National Lottery tickets. Over all, in the vast hot closeness of the market, hung a faint odor of decay and human feces.

Harley and Jim pushed their way among the heavy throng and came out the other side of the market, squinting in the sudden, bright light.

A bell boomed loudly overhead. They looked up.

Blinding in the sunlight, the gold cupola of a church flashed in the sky. Women, their heads covered with dark shawls, and men, their broad straw hats held at the breast, were hurrying up the steps. The bell rang again, the sound straining down, mute and heavy in the narrow, crowded street. A woman, her head and body covered in a black shawl, her face like leather, her lips moving in silent prayer, her black eyes wet with tears and fixed intently on the cavernous dark doorway of the church, went down on her knees on the large paving stones. Now and then she paused to lean far forward, her brow touching the stones, her hands, cracked and brown, held tightly at her breast, as she moved clumsily on her knees, her body rocking from side to side, up the worn, long steps of the church.

As Jim and the sailor walked along there was the constant cry of, "Hey, *americanos!* Taxi?" Children ran at their heels and in front of them, running backwards, holding up little boxes filled with candy and trinkets for sale. Old women with large trays of artificial flowers clawed at their sleeves. And in clusters on every street corner stood the pimps, whispering to them as they passed, "You wanna girl? Hey, Tex! Poosy?"

Soon the shops thinned out; there were fewer people on the streets. Presently, hardly anyone called to them or ran after them. They had come to the edge of town where the wooden sidewalks ended and the streets became spindly trails winding up into the low hills. Out on the baking desert were scattered dozens of huts made of the rusting Coca-Cola signs and corrugated sheetmetal. As they walked along, in the dark doorway of one, they saw a woman sitting on a chair, its straw bottom busted out, drying and combing her long black hair in the sun.

She had thrust the thick wet tresses down over her face and, with her heavy arms lifted, combed slowly and rhythmically downward and outward in even, unbroken strokes. The two men stopped and watched. The woman bundled a mass of her hair into her fist, swept it over one shoulder and began combing again with the motion of a bird stretching its wing wide and brushing its wing along the ground. Her hair had the shine of a bird's wing, glossy and rich.

The yard was a scorched garden with jagged rows of nubby plants pushing up out of the cracked earth in front of the hut. Behind the hut a goat was tethered to the branch of a squat bush. The sailor leaned a hand on the sagging, broken fence, its stick-like palings weather-silvered and mended and patched over the years with bits of rope and twine. Jim took out his handkerchief and wiped the sweat from the back of his neck.

The woman saw the men and stopped to stare at them, her comb poised over her hair. She smiled and let the comb fall to her lap. Letting her heavy thighs sag and spread, she tilted her head to one side and lifted her skirts high with one finger. All the time she was smiling at them and cocking her head pertly from one side to the other.

The flesh of her legs hung loose and pebbled in the stark afternoon sunlight, the skin greenish and laced with clusters of veins.

"Naw, that don't look so good," said Harley. Then, louder, to the woman, "You don't look good."

Jim tried to speak but his throat was parched with dust. He swallowed silently and shook his head, brushing the air foolishly and rapidly with his balled handkerchief. He stared down at his broken shoes, then stuffed the handkerchief into his pocket. Both men backed away from the fence. As they moved down the dusty shoulder of the road, the woman gave an indifferent wave of her arm and pushing down her skirts, dropped her hair over her eyes once more and resumed her combing.

The men wandered slowly through the streets for the rest of the afternoon, stopping now and then at a cantina for a bottle of beer or a glass of tequila and gorging themselves on heavy, greasy tacos. At one cantina, down in a dank cellar where the walls were cold and sweating and the toilet was a gaping smelly hole in the stones of the floor, Harley had started showing off, dancing around the edge of the hole as he relieved himself and would have fallen in if Jim hadn't knocked him back quickly against the wall.

As dusk fell they found themselves once more closer to the center of the town. There was a lightness in the air as though the burning sky of the day had sprung back from the heat-flattened earth.

They entered the broad main road. This area, still fairly close to the edge of town, wasn't so congested, but even so a few old, beat-up taxis were parked here and there at the curbs, the drivers leaning out and speaking softly to the soldiers and sailors who straggled along the cracked, uneven paving stones, peering into the gloomy doorways of the bars.

One man leaned out of his cab window and called to Jim and Harley. "We got blondes," said the driver, grinning and winking up at them. "Long legg-ed American blondes."

They stopped and stared at him, then Jim

scoffed, "Spics with wigs," and gave an indifferent flap of his hand.

But the sailor gripped his arm. "Whadda' ya' say, though?"

Jim tucked his hands in his hip pockets and stared off down the darkening street. "Prol'ly take us somewhere and roll us."

"Nobody'll ever roll *me*," said the sailor, sucking in his gut. Grabbing his jumper in his meaty fists, he snapped it down smartly over his expanded chest.

"Hey, *americanos!*" the cabman whispered. They both leaned down into the cab window. "You like boys? We got boys."

"Yeah, man! Where's the queers? I could go me a nice fifteen-year-old virgin boy!" roared the sailor, and slapped Jim heavily on the back.

The taxi driver stuck his arm out the window and snapped his fingers quickly. "Pst! *Señorita!*"

Out of the shadows of the arcade stepped a boy of no more than seventeen. He approached them smiling and with an undulant rolling of his slender hips. He wore tight black trousers and through his unbuttoned shirt front was a fine gold chain with a cross resting on his smooth, hairless chest.

Coyly ducking his head, the boy blinked his heavily mascaraed eyes up at Jim and Harley. The sailor bent at the knees and resting his hands on his kneecaps stared into the boy's face.

"You really a boy?"

"I *señorita*," giggled the boy and turned away shyly.

The sailor grinned and straightened up. The boy flashed a grin back at him, arching his supple body and, half turning, rose on his toes and dusted his slim buttocks lightly. Then he laughed and putting the chain of his necklace into his mouth, began lick-

ing the cross while he looked from one face to the
other.

The sailor drew Jim to the curb and whispered to
him, "Wanta give it a try?" He squinted his eyes, sur-
veying the boy. " 'Fraid I might kill him, though."

Jim snorted and kicked out with his heel. "There
you go, bragging again."

"Hell I am!" roared the sailor, punching Jim between the shoulder blades so that Jim almost fell
into the street.

Then a thoughtful expression came over the sail-
or's face and he rubbed his chin slowly for several
moments.

"It ain't—it ain't *natural*, damn it!" he burst out
at last and turning abruptly, almost with violence,
shouted at the boy, "G'wan, git outa here, ya' little
faggot! Vamoose!"

The cabman said something to the boy in Span-
ish and the boy, with a sudden expression of con-
tempt on his face, spit quickly on the sidewalk in
the direction of the pair and with a toss of his head
minced back among the darkened pillars of the market.

"I see you guys are real men, eh?" said the driver.
"You know," he said, with a shrug and loose wave
of his hand, "some guys like that—for a change,
you know?" He leaned closer to the men and whispered, "I got the woman for you, though."

"How much?" said Harley.

"Fi' buck. Ten all night."

"Whatta' ya' say?" said the sailor, leaning an
arm on Jim's shoulder and talking quietly in his
ear. "We don't like 'er, we don't have to stay. Let's
give 'er a lookover."

"Anything'd look good to me."

"Hey, call back that li'l sassy-assed boy!" shouted the sailor, and giving Jim a shove they got into the cab.

They drove off with a lurch and at great speed down the main street, past the neon-lighted bars and strip joints and souvenir shops. The sidewalks were packed now with the sailors and marines and soldiers who barreled in and out of the bars drunkenly, arm in arm, holding each other loosely, whooping and hollering. Pimps stood in tight groups at every street corner. The town police drove up and down the dusty street on their motorcycles, their baggy uniforms ballooning from their heavy bodies straddling the huge machines; large cumbersome-looking pistols strapped to their hips.

"Sure'n hell don't wanna' git in jail down here," said the sailor, peering anxiously over his shoulder out the rear window. "You git in the calaboose down here, buddy, you just rot. Even the U.S. Navy has a helluva time gettin' you out."

Soon the cab was out of the main district and zigzagged now up and down little side streets, at first past neat stucco bungalows with dusty lawns and tall, forlorn palm trees, then up into hills and down through a stretch of desert and higher wooded areas and finally through rutted alley-like streets where there was row after row of shacks with open ditches of foul water running in front of them. It was at one of these shanties at the end of a deserted dark road that the cab squealed to a halt.

The driver threw one arm over the back of the seat. "Go up and knock," he said, pointing to the dark hut. "Her name's Anita."

"She clean?" asked the sailor, bobbing his head about as he tried to make out the house.

The driver extended his palms. "Clean like an American woman."

Jim snuffled his nose. "Shit," he said.

"Whatta we owe?" Harley asked.

The Mexican shrugged and threw up his arms. "Fi' buck," he said.

"That all you greasers know?" snapped the sailor. "Here's three. That's all the ride was worth."

The cabbie rolled his shoulders philosophically as Jim and the sailor got out of the cab. "Wait'll we see if she looks good," said Harley, leaning in the window. "I'll give you the high sign."

The man nodded and Jim and the sailor stumbled up the dark yard and knocked at the door. There was the sound of bedsprings creaking, then bare feet slapping against earth and the sagging door opened, revealing the figure of a woman in silhouette against the dim, inner light.

"You 'Nita?" asked the sailor.

"*Sí*," the woman answered, nodding her head and eyeing the two strangers casually.

"That guy out there sent us," continued the sailor, jerking his head in the direction of the darkened cab.

"*Sí, sí*," the woman repeated. She swung the door open and the two men entered.

The room was small, lit by an oil lamp with a splintered globe hanging from a rafter of the ceiling and a flat, squat votive candle flickering in one corner beneath a calendar reproduction of the Virgin of Guadalupe.

The air was rancid with the stale smell of cooking and the odor of kerosene. There were a few broken cane chairs shoved against one wall and a three-legged table, the worn oilcloth of which was covered with flies and gave off a sour, milky odor.

Now and again the metal walls snapped and ping-ed as the cool air of the night took out of them the day's heavy heat.

The woman stood in the middle of the room, her flat black eyes watching the two strangers almost with indifference. She was dressed in a short, stained robe, belted loosely around the middle. She coiled and uncoiled the ends of the belt as she idly watched the men, a compactly built woman with her dark hair coiling about her face in looping, greasy ringlets.

"That's a pretty narrow workbench," whispered the sailor to Jim, eyeing the sagging metal cot in the corner of the room, its sheets and coverlet sweat-blackened and mottled with stains. Strewn and rumpled, the covers trailed on the earthen floor and bunched up against one corrugated wall.

"You don't do it back to back," said Jim, and nudged the sailor in the ribs. "How she look?"

"Okay."

The sailor stepped to the door and motioned for the waiting driver to go. There was the sound of the horn as the taxi pulled away down the road.

"Can't we get her to blow out that candle?" the sailor said aside to Jim. "Feels like a goddamned church in here."

"Wish it smelled like one."

The woman ran to the bed, gave the pillows a couple of hard thumps, fluffed them up, then turned and, letting her robe slip from her body to the floor, said, "Who firs'?"

"How much?" Jim said.

"Fife," she said. Then pointing to each, "Fife you —fife you." She held out her hand and the sailor whipped out his wallet and gave her a bill.

"This one's on me, pal," he said to Jim.

After neatly folding the money and tucking it under the votive light, she again turned to the men. "Who firs'?" she repeated.

The two men looked at each other.

"G'wan," said Jim, pushing the sailor toward the woman. "I don't mind sloppy seconds."

The sailor grinned, looking at the woman, and rubbed one finger briskly under his nose. He reached out for her, grabbing her bearlike into his arms and lifted her to the bed.

Jim walked to the door of the hut and stepped out into the night. The air had a soft, cool fragrance and was very still. The stars were tight-packed in the heavens and threw a faint light down into the valley. To the north, the glow of the town lit up the hilly horizon and farther to the south was the glow of the rising moon behind the hills.

Inside, he could hear the bedsprings beginning to creak loudly now and the amorous groans of the sailor. He stepped away from the door and lit a cigaret. There were footsteps moving softly and swiftly somewhere out on the dark road. Jim tensed, listening, and moved quickly out of the light of the doorway. Presently, the small, bundled figure of a Mexican loped past the house, now and again casting quick glances over his shoulder as he silently wheeled two automobile tires along with either hand.

There came the raucous squealings of the sailor within the hut, followed by a long, loud laugh, then silence. Jim stared again into the darkness but the Mexican had disappeared into the shadows of the road with his tires.

He felt a hand on his shoulder. It was the sailor standing in his skivvies and socks. "She's good, boy," came the elated whisper of the sailor in his ear. "I got 'er warmed up for ya'."

Jim pitched his cigaret into the drainage ditch and turned to go in at the doorway.

"Here, mate," said the sailor in the same stealthy, excited whisper. "Thought you might want this, 'case you're out."

He pressed the tightly packed ring of rubber into Jim's hand and clamped Jim lightly on the shoulder. "Man, I gotta take a wicked one." He walked toward the side of the hut and stretching his long arms wide to the sky, gave a great, loud yawn.

Jim went in, pushing the door to behind him. The woman lay on the bed. She had pulled the rumpled sheets above her waist but he could see her breasts, full and dark-nippled, in the gleam of the votive light. Trickles of sweat ran down her face and neck and flattened the black curls tight against her forehead.

"You hurt?" she said, pointing to the blood-stained shoulder.

He ducked his head sideways, craning down, seeing the stain as though for the first time.

"That? No."

"What you do?"

He held up his fists, poking the air as though he were boxing. He danced toward the bed.

"Oh!" she cried, sitting bolt upright and clapping her hands. "You win?"

"No."

She leaned over and ran her fingers down his cheeks, then moved her body closer to the wall and patting the space beside her, said, "Sleep?"

Jim dropped his clothes and got on the bed. As he climbed over her he could hear the sailor urinating against the metal wall of the shack, the sound of it reverberating in the room like buckshot thrown against it.

When it was over, and he had his face still buried in her hair, his body drenched with sweat, Jim loosened his clenched fist and found the contraceptive the sailor had given him, unused, in his hand.

The two made their way back to town, following as best they could the faint trace of the rutted, gully-like road under the light of the stars and keeping in the direction of the glow on the horizon, signifying the town.

The night air was suddenly cold, a dampish, flat cold, but now and again they walked through pockets of warm air that had the dry, brittle smell of day. There was a curious dense silence over everything, except for the occasional thin, high cry of a wild dog far off, up near the hills.

The road skirted woodland and presently the trees thinned to brush and the desert began, its sands sweeping off in the darkness to the distant hills. The hills were now crinkled and black against the light evening sky as a three-quarter moon rose behind them. Heavy stars hung near the crests, yet, far above, the sky was a fine rake of stars. Here and there gleamed lights of houses on the hills. There were the headlamps of a jitney bus, its tiny, jolting shafts of light illuminating shards of raw rock as it struggled up a ravine, the roar and cough of its motor coming muted over the distance.

Suddenly there were faint swishing noises from somewhere out on the desert. Jim and the sailor strained their eyes into the darkness to see. Along with the swishing sounds now came sharp yaps

and snarls, still low and far away. As the moon
lifted over the hills and threw its light upon the
plain, faint shapes of lean animals were visible lop-
ing in wide circles over the sand. The animals moved
steadily closer to them, their barks and snarls
sounding more distinctly on the still evening air as
the moonlight now fully illuminated the desert.

The two men stood fascinated, watching the wild
dogs trotting and leaping around and around. They
were fierce and hungry-looking animals. In the center of the circle were the bitches, their small,
pointed ears pressed flat against their narrow skulls,
tails stiff between their shivering legs, bunched together, backing into one another as they growled
and whined and lashed out with their teeth as a
male dog would leap in from the outer circle and
then swiftly leap back again.

The dogs swept by the boundary of the town,
their long bodies lifting and falling, the churning
animal flesh locked now in so tight a ring that the
bitches were completely hemmed in and no longer
distinguishable from the males. As the dark, snarling pack moved on, all that could be seen was a
thin, powdery cloud of dust rising slowly in the
moonlight. Their barkings and whinings became
muffled and lost and once again the night was still.

Jim sucked in his breath and let his shoulders
drop. The sailor was staring wide-eyed after the
cloud of dust. "They sure got some poor-looking
dogs down here," he murmured.

As they started walking again, Jim peered out
once more over the hills. The lights of the bus were
gone now; the moonlight softened the hills, taking
out of them the jagged brokenness of noonday.

The three Mexicans, when they stepped into the

road behind them, were, in the darkness, more felt by Jim than seen. They were not even shadows but a presence that Jim sensed which made him stiffen, alert, and then halt, laying an arm across the sailor's chest to stop him also. His eyes flicked out into the darkness. The sailor started, having now sensed the three men.

There was the click and fall of small stones and the soft crunch of gravel as they approached stealthily. Then they crept so close Jim and Harley could smell their dried sweat and the sharp, gasoline like odor of tequila.

There was a swift whisper of movement as two of the Mexicans sprang forward, locking an arm around each of the men's necks and pushing a knifeblade in his back, as the third Mexican leaped in front of the two and with quick, light hands began ferreting through the pockets of the sailor. Harley abruptly lifted one knee, catching the Mexican in the point of the jaw. There was a slight popping noise, like a small, thin shell cracked between the fingers, and the Mexican fell away into the darkness. In almost the same movement, the sailor reached his heavy arms behind his head, grasped the neck of the Mexican holding the knife against him, and with a lunge forward flung him over his shoulder, snatched him around by the shirtfront to face him and plunging back his arm, smashed him in the face. The little man sighed and dropped to the ground in a heap, still clutching his knife.

Meanwhile, Jim had been wrestling in the roadway with the last Mexican. They were rolling over and over in the dust. There was the sound of their short, hard breaths and muttered curses as they struggled. Jim finally got the Mexican flat on his back, his arms spread and pinned against the earth with his knees. Harley walked over and put his foot on the Mexican's arm, the one holding the knife, and slowly, with increasing pressure, ground his heel into the flesh of the Mexican's wrist. The Mexican writhed and squealed in pain, but Jim kept him pinned tightly to the ground, and a moment later the fingers grasping the handle slowly uncoiled as the heel of the sailor ground in harder, and the knife dropped in the dust. Harley snatched it up and heaved it as far as he could into the spidery, dust-choked brush at the side of the road.

Jim got off the Mexican and pulled him up by the arm, then swinging him around, gave him a hard kick in the behind. The Mexican, his body bending outward, flew off a yard or so, staggered, dropped to his knees, glanced wildly over his shoulder, then picking himself up ran off into the night.

Jim and Harley watched him disappear. They were both breathing heavily and stood quiet in the middle of the road. Then Harley stepped over to one of the unconscious Mexicans lying in the road and kicked him hard in the skull. The thin hands of the man flicked up for an instant, then fell clumsily into the folds of his shirt and were still.

After a moment the sailor said, "They hurt you?"

"Naw."

"Them goddamn Mex's is all chicken shit," said the sailor, and spat furiously over his shoulder, wiping his mouth with the back of his hand. "Looka' these whites," he muttered. He started slapping hard at his thighs and buttocks, raising clouds of dust from his uniform. "SP's'll have my ass for sure. I know a easy way to the hotel, though. Then we better light back across the border."

They started walking again. The road wound up one of the hills. Presently the trees dropped away. There was the broad sky and the sense of a great height, as though they had come to the top of the world. Down below, in the gathering light, the luminous trunks of the trees rose like dark snakes on the slopes.

"Dawn soon," said the sailor.

Jim grunted. "Let's jog," he said, and they started the swift descent back down into the town.

The Pipe

Five men stood around the mouth of the big corrugated pipe. The length of the pipe, propped on wooden planks bolted crosswise, stretched in a wavering line over the flat, sun-baked mud of the land, dipped about a hundred yards on over the edge of the bluff and could be seen, from where the men stood, trailing in a thin, black line across the beach far below and running on stilts out over the water to the dredge-boat anchored in mid-river. The sky was light green from the intense heat of a sun that beat down unmercifully on the broad level land. Flat acres of bleached clay, hardened and cracked in huge irregular slabs curled at the edges, billowed up heavy waves of shimmering, colorless heat. A flock of chicken hawks, wings taut and motionless, wheeled slowly high overhead. There was not a tree or a cloud in sight. The men were silent. Their rubber boots sank ankle deep into the mud and when a man shifted from one foot to the other, his boots made sucking noises. The mud spread in a wide pool around the mouth of the pipe.

One of the men, Alex, his face dark brown under the brim of his hat, pulled out a pocket watch. He glanced at the dial, then snapped the lid shut and thrust the watch back in his pocket. Shading his eyes with one hand, he looked out over the river to where the dredge-boat lay anchored.

"What time is it?" Carp said.

"The blow's just about due."

"I wish to hell they'd hurry it up. I'm sweating my balls off. Not a breeze. No nothing."

Carp's face and hands were burned red from the sun. The skin was peeling from his cheeks and around his neck. He kept picking off pieces of the loose flesh and rolled them into little balls between his thumb and forefinger. He dropped these pellets in the mud between his boots.

"Just be patient," Alex said. "You'll work yourself into a lather over it. Get yourself a sunstroke to boot. Why can't you be patient, like Billy there."

Billy glanced up. He was tall and thin and hatless.

"Billy's simpleminded," Carp said. "He don't feel anything. What do you feel, Billy? What're you feeling now?" he called.

"Don't torment the boy," said Alex.

"I'm a chicken hawk," Billy said, rolling his eyes to the sky.

The men chuckled.

"You see? He's a chicken hawk," Carp said. "It don't make sense."

"Billy's a queer bird all right, all right," laughed Ruby. He was short and fat and had a red bandana knotted around his throat. He wore a wide leather kidney belt with a big silver buckle and studded with brass rivets. There was a big floppy felt hat on his head that covered half his face.

"I'm a chicken hawk," Billy repeated.

"Hey, Billy, like this?" Ruby started flappping his arms like a bird.

"Never you mind."

Ruby laughed fluttering his arms, his belly shaking. He winked at Billy. Billy looked away.

"Me and you, Billy," he chuckled. "Birds of a kidney."

His face went scarlet with laughing and he had a fit of coughing and turned away, doubled up and still laughing, and fanned his face with his hat.

The men grew silent, watching the dredge-boat out on the river. Carp tore a long layer of skin off the back of his neck and began rolling it between his fingers. Bunk and Sam were standing off a little from the others. Bunk had his thumbs hitched in the loops of his belt and was sliding the sole of his boot back and forth over the mud. On his upper lip was a sore that a couple of flies buzzed around. He kept reaching up with his hand, brushing them away. Sam was big, with broad shoulders and thick arms and legs. His face was red and sweating and his dull eyes gazed listlessly out over the water.

Billy walked away from the group, beyond the pipe to where an old mud-spattered chevvy stood, its back seat torn out and that place jammed with rusty pieces of odd-shaped metal, piled almost to the ceiling and jutting out the windows. On either side of the chevvy was a handcart and a wagon made of orange crates, each filled with a couple of pieces of mud-caked metal. There were two burlap bags lying near the cart and wagon, and they were yellow with dust and bulging slightly. Billy sat down in the shade on the runningboard of the car. His cheeks were flushed and he was breathing heavily. He ran his fingers through his sweaty hair, then propped an elbow on one knee and cupped his chin in his hand.

"Penny by penny," he gasped. "Bye and bye."

"Them hawks make me nervous," snapped Carp. "Wisht to hell they'd go away."

He picked up a stone and flung it at the sky.

"You'd have to have a damned good arm to hit one of them birds," said Alex. He pushed back his hat and wiped the sweat from his brow with a piece of flannel.

"They get on my nerves, swimming around and around up there, like they could wait forever for something dead. I wisht they'd go away."

"I'll tell them to go away, Carp," Billy said, grinning and looking up open-mouthed at the hawks. "If you want me to, Carp."

"Whatta you going to do, fly up?"

"Sure, Carp. I can talk to them."

"You're loco, Billy."

"The heat's got him," Sam said.

"No I'm not, Carp. I can fly up there and talk to them and tell them to go away if they're bothering you. Honest I can, Carp."

"Well, you go on, Billy."

"Sprout wings," snorted Ruby.

"Not today, Carp."

"Why not?"

"It's too hot."

"Smart bird."

"I'll do it tomorrow, Carp."

"Okay. That's a promise."

"I learned when I was a baby."

"Sure, Billy."

"Billy, you oughta get yourself some kind of cap," said Alex. "The sun'll affect you coming out here bareheaded."

"It's affecting him already," Ruby said. "You hear how he thinks he can fly."

"I got a cap of silver and diamonds," Billy said. "But it's too good to wear out here."

"Listen to it, will you?" sneered Carp. "Billy,

you're a grown man. You oughta have more sense'n to talk like that."

"Well, I do. I bought that cap in New York City. You can't say I didn't."

"You're just making it up. When was you ever in New York City?"

"Never you mind. I'm gonna get a cap of gold next. When I get enough junk out of that pipe, that's what I'm going to do. I'm not kidding."

"Okay, Billy," Carp guffawed. "You show me."

"Well, I will."

"Whatta you do for a woman, Billy?" Ruby shouted.

"Let the boy alone," said Alex.

Carp yelled, "Oh, I bet he has wild nights with hisself, don't you, Billy?"

Billy giggled and pulled his hand over his eyes.

"The world's topsy-tursy, ain't it, Billy?" Ruby was shaking with laughter, the brim of his hat flopping up and down.

Billy snatched the hand away from his eyes.

"Why, no, sir."

"But you see things different from most people."

Billy hugged his knees with his arms, then said, "The world's round. Everybody knows that. But here," he said, his eyes moving slowly over the land, "it's flat as a checkerboard. God's lying."

"Now you be careful, Billy."

"Of what?"

"The Judgment Day. Talking about God like that, calling God a liar ain't healthy."

"It don't scare me none."

"Listen to him talk!" howled Carp. "Talking awful high and mighty, ain't you? You still a chicken hawk?"

Billy stared down at the mud.

"Don't tease me, Carp."

"I'm not teasing. I just want to know if you're still a chicken hawk, that's all."

"Well, I am if you want to know," Billy said angrily. "And tomorrow I'll fly up and tell them they annoy you."

The men burst out laughing. Bunk rubbed his hands agitatedly up and down his thighs, beating clouds of dust from his dungarees.

"Billy, you do take the cake!" he shouted.

"And I eat it, too. I like cake."

The men roared. Alex bent down at the mouth of the pipe and stuck his head in sideways, listening.

"What're they saying?" Sam asked, inching up close to Alex.

"One guy says, 'Lay off the chains'—That means the blow's about due. One guy's calling another one a bastard."

"He should if it's his fault the blow's late," Carp said.

"Something must be holding them up," Ruby said. "I sure wisht they'd hop to it. I feel like I'm being fried in deep fat."

"Well, if you feel that way, it's your own you're sizzling in," said Carp.

"Look here, Mr. Dry Bones, you're so thin I can smell the—"

"Shut up," Sam snapped. "Alex, what else they saying?"

"Nothing but racket. Nobody saying anything." Alex ducked out from the pipe and straightened up, squaring his hat straight on his head.

"Oh, come on, you last blow of the day!" Carp shouted, shaking his fist at the dredge-boat. "I want to get to Tarkie's, ditch my junk, and have me a cold bottle of beer."

"Go on and take a swim," Alex said. "Cool off."

"Not in that stinking water."

Ruby held his fingers to his nose and said, "Go on, Carp, go take a bath and give us a break."

"Be like a chemical bath," Bunk said. "Besides, the river's black with polio."

"That's Nigger Buddy's blood," Billy said, from the running board of the car. "Nigger Buddy made the river black."

"Who's Nigger Buddy?"

"You never heard of Nigger Buddy?"

"No, I never did. Another one of your stories I guess."

"Tell them, Carp. Tell them about Nigger Buddy Carson the day he went swimming off Blower Rocks. He made the river black."

"He did no such thing," Carp said. "He never made the river black."

"What happened? Come on, Carp, tell us."

"It ain't nothing much. Hardly worth telling."

"Come on. I bet it's something good. You're being selfish keeping it to yourself."

"Oh, it's good all right," Billy said, leaning forward and rubbing his hands together. "It's the reason the river's why it is."

"Talk about the river black, Mr. Bill Big-Lie," Carp said, turning on him. "I'd like to get a squint at that soul of yours. There can't be a shade difference'n you and the river the lies you jaw."

"Well, tell them, Carp. Let them judge for themselves."

"He never *got* to the water, I tell you. He took a low dive on the rocks and smashed his head open.

They had to scrape his brains off with a piece of cardboard."

"Was his brains black?" Billy said. "I never seen a nigger bare. What's it look like, Carp?"

"Carp can't tell you," Sam said, grinning and showing his long yellow teeth. "He dreamt the whole thing up."

"It's true. I was there. Seen it with my own two eyes!"

"Tall tales, tall tales," Sam sneered. "What was you doing, hiding in the grass and peeking at a naked nigger? I don't know what to think of that."

"I was fishing a little way off, you fool. You think I'm hot to see a boogie's dingle, the way Billy is?"

"What color is it, Carp?"

"Honest to God, Billy—"

"He'll tell you it's zebra-striped," laughed Sam. "Go on, tell him, he's so hot to know—zebra-striped with purple polka-dots."

"I'm telling you, Sam, I saw it all. You calling me a liar?"

"Answer my question, Carp."

"Tall tales," howled Sam, slapping his thigh. "Just more of your plain long-legged lies!"

"I'm warning you, Sam."

"Sam, you zipper your trap," Ruby said. "Let Carp go on and tell the story."

"Was it really black, Carp?"

"Let Carp tell us how many drinks he had beforehand," Sam chuckled. "Go on, Carp, tell us."

"Nary a one. I tell you, his brains was splattered all over them rocks. They had to pick off the pieces with a fork."

"Now it's forks. Oyster forks I guess, huh?"

"What's an oyster fork?"

"An oyster fork!" Carp snarled, turning on Ruby with such violence that Ruby backed away. "You mean you never heard of an oyster fork?"

"No, I haven't. I'm ashamed to say I never knew an oyster had one."

"Why, oysters don't grow them, you fool," Carp spluttered, his face reddening. "That's a fork for spearing oysters at highfalooting dinners. I seen plenty when I used to waiter down in Atlantic City."

"What's Atlantic City like, Carp?"

"You mean there's more than one kind of fork, outside of a pitchfork?" Ruby said, squinting at Carp and spitting a wad of tobacco juice plop in the mud.

"Why sure. Everybody knows that. First off, there're forks for olives. Now, you see, the rich got it all pretty complicated. I say *forks* for olives, 'cause there's forks for black olives, and forks for plain green olives (them with the pits still in), and then there's forks for olives stuffed with red gut. And, you see, you gotta know these things, else when you sit down to table and look baffled a minute at that long line of forks, people'll know you're dumb and not the ritz at all. They laugh at you behind their hands. I seen it happen."

"You know the difference between all these forks, huh?" Sam said. "You could put your knees under any fancy table and stick the right olive with the right fork, huh? You could do that?"

"Why sure. Didn't I used to waiter in a lush hotel? I watched and learned them things."

" 'Case you get rich someday, huh?"

"In case. Now you take oyster forks," Carp said, turning to Ruby. "Same thing there."

"Oh God, here it comes!"

"No, you listen," Carp said over his shoulder to Sam. Then to Ruby, "There's a fork for Blue Point oysters and a fork for Pawtucket oysters and another for Queen of Sheba oysters and then one for Jersey oysters—A fork for all the kinds of oysters in the world."

"Aw, come on. How they have room on the table for all them forks?"

"Oh, they have room," Carp said, not looking at Sam. "Big, grand table. 'Course, they don't serve *all* the oysters in the world at one sitting."

"'A course not. Nor all the olives, I bet."

Carp turned and eyed Sam haughtily, folding his arms across his chest.

"Well, there's more kinds of oysters than olives," he said. "You got more forks to remember with oysters. Olives is easy. But the most pretty fork of all the oyster forks is a eensy-beensy silver one, all kinds of loops and curls carved on it, and the handle studded with diamonds. They usually have a couple of them on every table. Just in case."

He paused, smiling mysteriously through Sam. Sam watched him, waiting, but Carp kept on smiling and didn't say anything. Finally Sam said, "In case of what?"

Carp stopped smiling and stared at him blankly, as though he hadn't seen him before.

"I beg your pardon?"

"Don't give yourself airs," Sam grumbled. "I say, in case of what?"

"Was you referring to them special eensy-beensy silver oyster forks I was mentioning a couple of minutes ago?"

Carp drew himself up grandly.

"You know damn well I am."

"Well," Carp drawled slowly, flicking a speck of imaginary dust off the tip of his nose, "they have a couple of them forks on each table just in case some lady or gent pokes into their oyster and strikes a pearl. Then right off, there's a lot of excitement and laughing, and the lady—I seen it happen to a lady once, barebacked she was with the prettiest little freckles on her shoulders—I seen it happen to her."

He paused, carefully inspecting his fingernails.

"What?" Sam said in a cracked voice.

Carp glanced up at him. "Why, just what I been talking about. She comes up with a pearl in her oyster. And, right off, she lays down her fork—Blue Pointers was served that night so it was a Blue Point fork—she lays that fork down and reaches over for the little fork studded with diamonds and scoops in under that oyster and brings up the prettiest pearl you ever seen—all soft silver and kind of glowing in the light of the chandeliers, and pure round as a marble. She held the pearl up on that special fork and showed everybody. And what a commotion was raised about how beautiful it was. The ladies started hollering to see it so they passed it around the table for everybody to take a good squint at. I tell you, it was stunning."

"Me, something like that was passed my way," Sam said gruffly, "I'd pocket both pearl *and* fork and go on nonchalant with my soup."

"You, you would. You don't know nothing about breeding and manners."

"But you do?"

"I ain't bragging. I can hold my own. But, you listen, didn't I have a chance to learn it with my own two eyes?"

"Lot of good it'll do you."

"You never can tell. I might cash in one of these days on this here dredge."

"Don't hold your breath. Better you go spearing oysters at fancy dinners."

"Don't you think I couldn't."

"Ha-ha."

"I may not know anything about manners," Ruby said. "But I can sure show you something about breeding."

"What's that?"

"You just match me with any woman, I'll show you the grandest blue-ribbon breeding you ever saw."

The men laughed.

"That ain't the kind of breeding I mean."

"There ain't no other kind, Carp. Not in my books."

"That just shows how dumb you are."

"Ruby laid the baby in the pipe."

"What're you talking about, Billy?"

"I know. I saw him do it. Alex, tell us how you found that baby in the pipe."

"Billy, I've told you that story a dozen times. I'd think you'd be sick of it by now. Besides, it's not a nice story to tell. It wasn't Ruby's baby anyway."

"It wasn't my baby," Ruby said.

"I'm not tired of it, Alex. I like it. Tell it again."

"Billy, you know that story as well as I do. Why don't you tell it?"

"I'm not very good."

"Get out," Carp said. "You know you're busting to tell it."

"Well, maybe I am. Shall I tell it, Alex?"

"I told you, Billy. I'd like to hear it. How 'bout you boys?"

"Go on, Billy. Do your stuff," Ruby said. "You can't be any worse than Alex."

"You be careful. I'll tell whose baby that was."

"I ain't done any cavorting. You can't blame that on me. That's a terrible thing to say, Alex."

"Well, just you mind how you criticize my story-telling."

"I was only funning."

"Shut up, you two," Sam said. "Spin it out, Billy."

"All right. But you mustn't laugh."

"I'll bust your nose you blame that baby on me."

"Shut your flap, Ruby. We know you ain't capable," Carp said. "Hey, Billy—Can we listen?"

"Why sure. How else? But you mustn't laugh."

"Can we look?"

"At me?"

"Who else?"

"Well, all right. But you mustn't laugh. If you laugh I can't tell it."

"I'll be a juke box feather plucked nigger of an angel," snapped Bunk. "Get on with it, Billy, for Jesus sake."

Billy walked over to the mouth of the pipe and stood very erect. He set his lips firmly and stared straight ahead of him.

"I'm ready," he said solemnly.

"Shall we draw the curtain, Billy?"

Billy looked around, flustered, then glanced uncertainly at Carp.

"Well, okay," he said finally. "You can do it now."

Billy watched as Carp took a gigantic stride forward, made a sweeping bow to the tips of his boots. He swung out his arm and, grazing Billy's nose with his hand, grandly pulled back an imaginary curtain. Turning, he bowed from the waist to the men, one hand clapped smartly on his hip. The men applauded and stamped their boots in the mud. Billy squirmed and wriggled, still at attention, and glanced impatiently at Carp, who continued bowing up and down and tipping his cap to the men. The men went on shouting and clapping.

"Now you got them laughing!" Billy shouted, red in the face and clenching and unclenching his fists. Carp paid no attention to him and as he bent down for another bow, Billy gave him a shove in the buttocks with his foot. Carp reeled around, dead pan, and slapping the heels of his boots together, gave Billy a smart salute.

"Sorry, Cap'n," he said, rubbing his backside.

"Scoot!" snapped Billy, shooing a hand at him.

Carp made another snappy salute, then marched stiff-legged over to the men, grinning, his face flushed. The others hooted and slapped him on the back.

"That was some show, Carp! That was all right!"

"Real fine acting, Carp! Real fine!"

"You want to hear this story or not?" Billy shouted, glaring at them.

"Oops, there's the curtain up and us ignoring the main actor," chuckled Ruby. He genuflected on one knee and blew a kiss to Billy. "Proceed. Proceed."

Billy took a step forward and shook his fist at Carp. "Damn you, Showoff, you spoiled everything!"

"I'm awful sorry, Cap'n," Carp said, pulling off his cap and hanging his head sheepishly. He twisted his cap around and around in his hands.

"Well, you spoiled it, Mr. Movie Star. I'm about ready to close this curtain and forget the whole thing."

"Aw, don't do that," Bunk pleaded.

"Men, here's the way," Carp said, turning briskly to the group and spreading his arms. His face relaxed in a serious and solemn expression. Ruby stifled a giggle behind his hand and settled down and grew quiet. They each put on a quiet, listening face.

"I'll do it now," Billy said.

He walked over to the pipe and leaned one elbow on it, crossing one foot in front of the other.

"Well, to begin—Alex was leaning on the pipe one day. Just like this. Huh, Alex?"

"That's right, Billy."

"It was terrific hot. The old sun burned a trillion billion watts a second."—He wiped his hand over his brow—"Just like now."—He glanced up at the sun—"Well, the old pipe here"—He gave it a terrific thump with his fist—"started chuckling and gurgling for the last blow. Alex steps back and waits."—He moved backward, folding his arms over his chest and glared steadily at the pipe—"Then the whole pipe begins jerking and dancing off its pins as the blow gushes close."—He started to leap in the air and flailed his arms about—"Then out she whooshes!" he shouted, and dove at the men who leapt back in alarm—"And there's a great explosion of water and mud and rock and junk a thousand feet high!" he screamed, the muscles in his throat red and swelling.

"Make it fifteen feet, Billy."

"Anyway," Billy gasped, licking his lips and stalking around, "the blow peters off—begins to sicken and fall."—He staggered back, his lids half drooping, one hand pressed to his forehead, lips quivering and teeth chattering—"And dies!"—He keeled over in the mud and lay still.

"Billy, you'll get your clothes all—"

"Then! Quick as a flash! Up he bounds!"—He scrambled to his knees—"And starts clawing through rock and mud for junk!"—He rooted savagely in the earth with his fingers, flinging stones and mud over his shoulder, his hair flying in his face—"He finds a good hunk—pitches it aside—and another."—He heaved a stone in the direction of the men—"Finds another—it's a real good day—coming in copper—a good blow—another good hunk!" The last stone struck Ruby's boot and Ruby let out a howl and began hopping around on one foot while holding the other in both hands.

"Hey, careful, Billy—"

"Then all of a sudden!"—Billy knelt back on his heels and lifted his arms in amazement. His eyes bulged from his head as he stared down terrified at a particular spot in the mud. His mouth hung open. The men crowded forward, craning their necks to see what he was looking at. He let out a long low cry and slowly pressed his fingers into his cheeks. Then, gently reaching down, he pulled an imaginary object from the mud. He held it aloft, shrinking from it and glancing sideways at it, his eyes rolling with terror.

"It was the baby," he whispered.

The men stared uncomfortably at Billy's outstretched hand.

"It's all mangled and black," he said, rising slowly from his knees. "You can hardly tell it is a baby. Black like a nigger. Black and bloated from the river." He pinched his nostrils with his fingers. "It stinks like fish in the sun. Nigger, it don't have no legs. Legs ripped up in the dredge or in the pipe. But maybe—" He clutched the baby under one arm and frantically searched the ground at his feet. "Maybe them two legs come out with the blow. Maybe they're buried here under all this mud and rock." He carried the baby over to dry ground and laid it down carefully. Then he raced back to the mouth of the pipe and going down on his hands and knees began scratching and digging through the mud. "Them legs might be here. They just might be."

Ruby hurried forward.

"Look there, Billy!" he said excitedly, pointing. "There."

"Where? Here?" Billy swung around. "Ah, here, huh?" He started tearing away in that place, searching. Finally he stopped and wiped the sweat off his face with the sleeve of his shirt. He stood up and peered at the earth, then over to the dry ground where he had laid the baby. "Not here. Nowhere. Not anywhere. No legs. Baby ain't got no legs. Baby gets buried without no legs." His shoulders were shaking and he started to cry. "No legs. Not anywhere." He looked up suddenly, snapping his fingers, his face brightening. He swung around and ran over to the pipe. Bending down, his hands gripping his knees, he stared grinning into the mouth of the pipe.

"Next gush!" he cried, his voice echoing inside the pipe. "Another blow—Maybe them legs'll turn up. I'll keep an eye out. I'll scratch the mud. I'll find them legs. Last thing I do, I'll find them baby's legs. I'll glue 'em back on."

He spun around, laughing, and danced a jig from foot to foot, clapping his hands over his head. "Next blow!" Abruptly he stopped and stood stiff and straight, his arms pressed tightly at his sides.

"Police come and take the baby." He fell to the earth and hopped around on his knees. "No legs. Baby ain't got no legs. Got wings, no legs." He scraped around in the mud. "Day after day—another—next blow—they don't turn up—mud, rock, junk—no legs—baby gone—no legs—oh, where could they be?" He jumped up and stood once more at attention, his heels close together, staring straight ahead of him. "Lord, I don't look anymore. I forget about it."

He looked down at his toes, wriggling them.

"Well, that's the way it went, wasn't it, Alex?"

"You done it a thousand times better, Billy." Alex blew his nose hard on the piece of flannel. "That was a very fine performance."

"There, that just closes it up," Bunk said, stepping over and drawing the curtain shut.

"You oughta go on Broadway," Ruby said.

"You think so?"

"You got talent. That was something to see, Billy, I'm telling you."

"Next time I go into New York City, I'll look into that. Where do you go?"

"I was at the Ziegfeld Follies once," Ruby said. "Let's see—" He rubbed his heavy cheeks. "That must of been twenty to twenty-two years ago. Mighty fine theater. Good show. You just go there. They'll fit you in."

"You think so?"

"I'm certain. You just do the act you did here for us."

"I'd have to practice."

"Well, practice."

"No, Ruby, I think I'd rather go to Hollywood. I like movies better."

"Do what you like. You're wasting your time in this desert. Whatta you want being a junkie?"

"I don't know, Ruby."

Billy was silent.

"You suppose somebody didn't want that baby?" Carp said, turning to Alex.

"What do you mean?"

"Well, say a fella gets a girl fixed good and them not being married or anything, they get rid of it tossing it in the river. Say maybe the girl has the baby off in the woods somewhere by herself and when it's born puts it in a paper bag, like what you get at the A&P, and carries it to the river and goodbye, trouble. Say maybe the boyfriend helps her."

"I don't know, Carp. Might be. I don't know where that baby come from."

"Well, if the boyfriend was to help her," Ruby said, "I think that it'd take plenty of nerve to dive into her again. I can't imagine wanting anything more to do with her. It's bad enough being in the same house when one of your kids is born. You listen to her howling like that and it makes you feel bad."

"But you forget," Sam said.

"Hell, yeah."

"That's why I hustle my old lady to the hospital every time. On account of the noise she makes. And the names she calls me when she's in the throes of it—'Alex, you bastard, you touch me again I'll kill you—So help me I'll cut it off—you nogood sonuvabitch, you got me like this—You touch me again I'll kill you.' Stuff like that. Hospitals, they take care of the scream and the mess. It's worth the money."

"It's hell to have to listen to. They're out of their heads."

"But they forget."

"Oh, sure."

"Thank God for that. That'd really be hell, eh, boys? I mean if they never forgot and would never let you touch them again after that."

"It ain't natural. Earth'd empty in no time. So you needn't worry."

"God provides," Billy said.

They laughed.

"I guess it's toughest on the women. What's that in the Bible—?"

"Now don't go spouting that stuff."

"No, but I mean there's something in there about woman. Goes—first the pleasure and then the pain. Then the whole thing all over again, never stopping. Us men are lucky—pleasure and more pleasure and never a worry about a day of reckoning."

" 'Cepting in case you get a dose of something."

"Well, I always say you should pick a wife clean when you pick her."

They all laughed.

"I didn't mean that. I mean when you're off on a toot and ain't careful. A man's gotta watch out he don't catch something."

"No, that's one thing can knock up a man."

"Put him out of commission—but good."

"Something a woman don't have to worry about. I read somewhere she can carry it and dose a man up proper, but it don't mean she's gonna bust out in sores and go blind."

"No, that's tough on a man."

They stared at Bunk's upper lip.

He grinned and pointing to his mouth said, "That ain't nothing. Just a cold sore."

"You can't be too sure," Sam said. "It looks funny to me, Bunk. Now I don't mean to say you're diseased or anything, but that scab of yours sure does look peculiar."

"It's nothing, I tell you."

"You've had that *cold* sore as long as I've known you, Bunk. That's been ten years."

Bunk shrugged his shoulders and jammed his hands into his back pockets. He turned away, shading his eyes with one hand, and looked over the river.

"Wonder when that blow's coming?" he said.

There was a silence. Then Alex said, "But a man's lucky, I will say that. He don't have to put up with the monthly bleed or be afraid of getting pumped full of baby every so often."

"You said the truth there," Sam said. "Let's have a drink on that. Whatta you say, boys?"

"I wouldn't throw *my* glove in the glass," chuckled Ruby, rubbing his hands together.

Sam took a whiskey flask out of his hip pocket and unscrewed the lid.

"Sam, can I have some?"

"A mouthful, Billy. Just enough to fill a cavity in a tooth. You know how rammy you get on a little whiskey."

"All right, Sam. I'll hunt the biggest cavity I can find."

"I don't mean your belly," Sam said, tilting the bottle to his lips. He took a long drink and rinsed it around in his mouth before swallowing it. He wiped his mouth on his sleeve and passed the bottle to the others.

"Pass Bunk by," he said, pulling out his penknife and scraping the dirt between his nails. "I don't want a man with a scab sore on his mouth sucking on my bottle."

Bunk ground his heel in the mud, then looked up

at the sky, watching the chicken hawks drift in big circles overhead. He glanced secretly at the others out of the corner of his eye. Carp had the bottle now and as he lifted it to his lips, Bunk saw muddy thumbprints smeared around the neck of it. His fingers moved up to his mouth and brushed away the flies buzzing there.

Suddenly the pipe began to vibrate and the men straightened up, tense and waiting. Ruby passed the bottle to Billy. Billy looked around at the men and they were staring at the pipe, so he took a long pull on the bottle, choking a little, then walked over and gave the bottle back to Sam. Sam held the bottle up in the sunlight, squinting one eye and making a peeved clucking noise in his throat as he measured the whiskey.

In the pipe was the sound of rock clanking against metal, the noise of it coming at a fast clip and growing steadily louder. Sam stepped forward, screwing the lid on the bottle, then thrust it in his pocket. He put his hands on his hips, watching the pipe and running the tip of his tongue over his lips.

"It's coming," Alex said.

" 'Bout time," said Carp, striding over and standing directly in front of the pipe, legs spread.

A faint roar came out of the mouth of the pipe, along with a steady gust of stagnant air. The men were silent, bearded jaws hanging slack on sunburned faces, and intense narrowed eyes hypnotized by the dark mouth of the pipe. The roar increased and the entire length of the pipe hummed and shook as though trying to free itself from the earth. There was the slosh and suck of water, and the blast of air pushing from the opening increased in pressure, flattening Carp's clothes against his body.

His hat blew off but he didn't move and stood rooted there, his arms folded tightly over his chest.

"It's cool!" he shouted. "Damned cool! But what a stink! Whew!"

"Get back, Carp! It's coming! It's coming!" Billy cried, hopping up and down behind the men. "It'll cut you to pieces! Drown you, Carp!"

Carp leaped aside. The men scattered. Billy started to run, but tripped and fell, sprawling face flat on the ground. Sam and Bunk ran back and each grabbed one of his arms and pulled him away from the pipe.

The black water pounded out like an explosion, shooting straight out, slapping the earth hard and driving up a wall of mud and rock before it, flattening the earth and pocketing it deeper with ton after ton of water.

The men stood at a distance watching. Billy had his back turned on the flood and was rubbing at a skinned elbow. Above the roar of the water they could hear the shrill whistle of the dredge-boat and looking, saw a cloud of black smoke billowing from the boat's stack. After a few minutes the whistle stopped blowing and gradually the column of water slackened, growing shorter until only a narrow steady gush spilled from the lip of the pipe.

The men dove forward, splashing kneehigh in the muck. Each bent down low, his bare arms slopping and stirring through the mud. As a man found a piece of pigiron or junk, he tossed it to dry ground, shouting, "Mine!" and went on dipping for more. Sam and Alex worked close together, several times bumping into each other. They each grabbed onto a piece at the same time. They glared at each other for an instant, then the mud rippled between their struggling arms as each tried to pull the object away from the other.

"It's mine! I found it first!" Sam shouted in his face, clenching his teeth and gripping the object tightly beneath the surface.

"No, mine! My hand touched first!"

"Liar! You're poking in my territory!"

"Your territory! Mine, you mean!"

"Let go!"

"I won't! I grabbed first. It's mine!"

"The hell you say. You drop that end. This piece belongs to me."

"Fight for it, boys!" Ruby yelled, quickly glancing over his shoulder, then bending down and slurping through the mud again.

"Drop yours. It's my prize. I touched first!" Sam bellowed.

"Touched first, hell!"

"Let go!"

"You let go!"

They began to tug hard on the object, pulling it halfway out of the mud. Sam gave a strong jerk and the object slipped from their hands, sliding back into the mud with a silent plop. Their arms splashed down in the mire as each fought to get hold of it again, their arms in deep to the elbows and their hands feeling and thrashing blindly. Sam plunged in to his shoulders and found an edge of the object.

"Damn you, Alex, I'm warning you. I got it for certain this time."

Alex crouched in the mud.

"I got my end too, goddamn you. I ain't letting you cheat me."

"Nobody's cheating. You're the goddamn cheater. You always was a cheat, Alex. Everybody knows that."

Alex let his end of the object drop. Sam pitched forward under the weight and he dropped his end, the object disappearing under the surface. He made a grab for it and Alex reached out and gave him a shove on the shoulder. He slowly placed his hands on his hips, scowling at Sam.

"You say that again," he said quietly.

Sam glared at him, breathless, his mouth hanging open, his face blood red and sweating.

"You're a cheat!" he shouted, straining forward. "Everybody knows it."

Bunk and Ruby and Carp swung around and stared at the two men. Billy went on splashing around in the mud, beating his arms through it and snatching up hunks of slimy pigiron.

"Once more," Alex said, wading closer. "Just tell me that once more."

"Once is enough," Sam said, inching backward and looking awkwardly away. He stumbled and caught his balance, then lifted his head and stared straight at Alex. "I don't have to call you a cheat three times to let you know it."

Alex stopped, gritting his teeth, and eyed Sam up and down. Then, swinging his arm back as far as it would go, he shot it forward, slamming Sam's jaw with all his strength. Sam groaned and his eyes rolled up in his head as he toppled backward in the pool of muck. Alex snatched him around the throat before he went under and dragged him to dry ground. Sam struggled to get free as Alex swung back his fist again. Sam's lips were quivering and he peeled at the mud on his cheeks as he stared into Alex's face. Alex held him by the shirt buttons, like a limp thing, his lower lip jutting and snarling, holding his arm back, when Sam suddenly wrenched loose and bounded away, falling and dragging himself through the dust. He stopped a few yards away and looking back at Alex, dug a rock out of the ground and held it clenched in his hand.

"Come one step more, Alex, I'm warning you," he choked.

"You wanta throw rocks?" jeered Alex. He glanced quickly around, spotted Billy's mound of pigiron and snatched a crude metal flange, still wet and muddy, from the heap. He came at Sam with the flange held tight in his fist, the jagged end out.

"I'm warning you," Sam gasped, dragging himself away from Alex. "I'm warning you."

Alex stood over him.

"Get up."

Sam struggled to his feet, slowly raising the rock in one hand as he lifted himself. He had pulled himself up into a stooped position, the rock held high over his head, when Alex shouted, "Me, cheat! You nogood bastard!" and walloped Sam's head with the metal flange, ripping a chunk of the skull away. Sam crumpled in a heap and lay still. The rock had flown from his hand and landed a few feet away, raising a cloud of dust where it struck the earth. The men stood in the mudhole staring, their arms hanging loose at their sides. Billy gaped, one arm pressed across his belly and the fingers of his other hand stuffed in his mouth. Alex turned his back on them and still holding the bloody flange in one hand, stared down sullenly at his muddy boots.

"Me, cheat!" he gasped.

Billy floundered out of the mud, kicking his legs high. He started to run toward Alex but stopped a few feet from him and began rubbing his hands up and down his thighs. He bit his lip and jerked his head back, to where the men were standing. He tried to call to them but could not raise his voice. The three men glanced uneasily at each other, then waded slowly out of the water. When they got on dry ground, each stamped his boots vigorously, knocking off the mud. Bunk stamped the longest and finally he stopped and the three stood, hands in pockets, uncomfortably looking at Alex and then at the dead man and back at Alex.

"What're you going to do, Alex?" Billy whispered.

Alex did not answer but remained standing with his back to them.

"You didn't have to do that, Alex," Carp said. "You didn't have to go that far."

"Sam didn't mean it," Bunk said. "He was out of his head."

"He was afraid of you, Alex."

There was silence. Billy lurched forward, his body loose and stooped, his mouth open. He was staring wide-eyed across the land.

"What's the matter, Billy?"

Alex swung around.

"He's in a temper," he said. "Billy, come out of it. Don't do that. I'll take you home in my car."

Billy's throat worked rapidly, his adam's apple bobbing up and down. His tongue fluttered noiselessly over his dry lips. He lifted a hand and pointed in the distance.

"More of your tricks?" Carp snapped. "More of your tricks? Whatta you see?"

Billy's arm was trembling, his body shook from head to foot.

"Them men in black!" he spluttered. "They're coming this way with leather belts in their hands."

The men shielded their eyes and stared off hard

in the distance. There was the broad expanse of land running unbroken the length of the horizon, ash-white in the heat, and empty.

"There's nothing out there but mud—"

Alex turned away, passing a hand over his face. He pulled his hat low over his eyes.

"Give him some water. Christ, somebody—"

"They're passing against the sky," Billy said thickly, his eyes dull and listless. A dribble of saliva ran down his chin. "They dropped the straps. The casket's gray."

"Shut up, Billy!" snapped Carp angrily. "This ain't no time for that kind of nonsense."

"But where're they going? Where're they gonna bury the casket here? The mud's too hard for digging. I'd better go tell them. They'd better go take that casket some place else."

He took a few steps forward and stopped, pressing his knuckles into his eyes. "Where're they going?" he said softly.

Carp sprang to him and spun him around, grabbing him tight by the shoulders.

"Softhead! Softhead!" he screamed in his face.

"Don't hurt me, for godssake, don't—"

Carp shook him violently.

"Shut up! Shut up!"

"Let him alone," Alex said. "He's sick. Let him alone."

"Carrying on with your tricks after what's happened," Carp sneered.

He gave Billy a shove, pushing him away, and turning on his heel, strode angrily back to the others. Billy tottered a moment, lifted his hand to his face, his eyes rolling wildly in his head, then suddenly pitched forward, diving flat on the ground close to Alex and lay there kicking his legs and muttering and growling, his knuckles digging frantically into the earth. Alex leapt back as Billy's arm shot out, his hand clamping tightly around Alex's ankle. He continued to squirm and writhe on his belly and beat the other fist in the dust.

"It's a clamp of steel!" Alex cried. "Bust his fingers loose! He's stopping the blood in my foot! He'll snap the bone!"

None of the men made a move. Beads of sweat stood out on Alex's brow, his eyes darted from one silent face to the other, then down at the hand squeezing his ankle in a death grip.

"Are you going to stand there like dummies?" he cried. "He's breaking my leg!"

The men were silent, staring with fascination at the thin figure rolling in the dust.

Alex glanced at the metal flange that he still held in one hand. He looked at the men then quickly bent down and whacked Billy's fist again and again with the bloody end of the flange. Billy held on tight. Alex beat harder until the white, tense knuckles were slashed and raw. He kicked his leg back and the hand fell away, striking the earth, the fingers uncoiling in a pool of blood and dust. Billy lay still, on his side, the arm flung over his head.

"Damn fool!" Alex gasped. "Damn fool, you!"

He tossed the flange as far as he could throw it.

"You oughtn't to done that," Ruby said. "That's evidence."

"Evidence?"

Alex stared at him.

"You know what I mean."

Alex glanced quickly at the dead man, then turned hastily away, breathing heavily. He pulled out the piece of flannel and mopped his face.

"I guess I'll go in my car now," he said, stuffing

the rag back in his pocket. "I guess I'll drop Billy off at his house first."

He watched the faces of the men, then stared at the ground, putting his hands awkwardly in his pockets.

"You'll know where to find me."

He lifted Billy in his arms and carried him over to the chevvy. Reaching under with one hand, he opened the door and set Billy on the seat. He slammed the door and crossed around to the other side, got in and started the motor. Billy sat unconscious, his head bumping and rolling from side to side on the dirty green felt of the backrest. Alex sat stiff and erect at the wheel, his eyes unblinking and staring straight out the windshield. As he turned the car north, Billy's head swerved off the seat and banged against the window sash. It rested there, one cheek bumping against the metal, his eyes closed and his mouth open and twisted to one side of his face.

The men watched as the car jolted slowly away, moving off in a straight line over the land and raising a slow steady cloud of dust behind it. They watched until the cloud of dust hid the chevvy, then turned and each looked for an instant at the dead body sprawled in front of the mouth of the pipe. The blood was drying and hardening in a brown crust where the piece of skull was ripped away. Flies crawled black in the wound.

Bunk clapped his hand over his mouth, then vomited in the mud. He looked up, embarrassed, wiping the puke from his mouth with the back of his hand.

The others moved over to where the sacks and the carts were.

"We can't let him lie here like this," Bunk said.

"You can't touch the body," Carp said, shoving the metal around and arranging it in the wagon. "They always tell you that."

"We got to go into town and tell the police," Ruby said. "That's all we can do."

"Well, oughtn't we to cover him?" Bunk said, glancing over his shoulder at the dead man. He shuddered and stared down at the earth. "It gags me. I mean, God, look at him."

Ruby and Carp were silent. They looked uneasily at each other.

"What can we do?" Ruby said.

"Dump the junk out of one of the sacks," Bunk said. "That's the least we can do. Keep the flies and sun off his head."

"Whose sack?"

"It don't matter. You or Ruby empty your sack. I'll carry your load in my wagon."

Ruby and Carp gazed silently at each other, then looked away, each scuffing a foot in the dust.

"I'll keep the junk separate. I won't mix it with mine or try to cheat you," Bunk said. "My God."

"Well, I'll do it," Ruby said. He pulled up the mouth of his burlap bag and dragged it over to Bunk's pushcart.

"Give a hand here, Carp."

Carp came over and together they emptied the bag of junk into the cart.

"Now bring the sack here," Bunk said.

"I'll pitch it to you."

"Well, all right. Pitch it."

Ruby wadded the bag into a ball and tossed it to Bunk. It fell a few feet from Bunk and Bunk walked over and picked it up and carried it to the mouth of the pipe. He unwadded it and turning his back on the dead man, gave the bag a couple of smart snaps, shaking it out. He moved his head to one side, not looking, as he prepared to spread the bag over the dead man, but he stopped and first leaned down to shoo the flies from the wound. The flies scattered, buzzing furiously. As soon as he lifted his hand away the flies once more infested the bloody cavity. He swiped at them again and again with his hand, but only a few flew off.

"Hustle it up, Bunk. You want to look at the thing all day?" Carp called.

"Come on, Bunk. Else we'll leave without you."

Bunk did not answer. Suddenly he darted his finger into the wound and worked it around and around in it, scraping away the wall of flies. The flies flew off in an angry swarm. He pulled the finger away and wiped it on the seat of his dungarees. Quickly he spread the burlap over the upper part of the body. He stared at a ragged hole showing a bit of the dead man's throat through the cloth. His hands moved swiftly over the ground, scooping in four small stones. He laid a stone on each of the four corners of the bag, then stood up and hurried over to where the men were waiting.

"What do you want to be so neat for?" Carp said. "He's dead ain't he?"

Bunk did not say anything but went to his pushcart. He laid a hand on each handle and tried to lift it, but the cart was too heavy.

"Carp, give a hand here. Ruby, you pull Billy's wagon."

Carp took hold of one of the handles and Bunk took the other. Together they lifted the cart and pushed it along. Ruby trudged behind, pulling the wagon of orange crates, his bag of junk sitting on top of the pile. They moved off in the direction of town, Bunk and Carp struggling with the cart over the ruts. Their footsteps sent up little balls of dust.

As they moved off over the land, the chicken hawks swooped in lower and smaller circles until they were flapping in tight rings just over the spot where the dead man lay, his long legs sticking out from the bottom of the burlap covering. The birds flew around and around, descending still lower in fluttering narrow loops until their wings brushed the burlap cloth. The air was filled with their harsh, agitated cries. When the men disappeared over the horizon, one of the hawks hurtled down and with a noisy flapping of its wings, alighted on the mouth of the pipe. One by one the hawks darted from the flock and dropped to the earth where they strutted in small circles, several bristling their feathers and crying sharply to one another, as they reeled and turned, hopping closer to the body of the dead man.

The Bar

Muskrat ran for the railing of the bridge, gripped it firmly in both hands, and swung himself over the side, dropping into the darkness below. He fell, his baseball cap flying off, in a sitting position on the embankment. He grabbed his baseball cap, picked himself up off the ground, dusting the seat of his dungarees, and scurried beneath the bridge, his hands stretched out in front of him as feelers. One arm glanced the side of an iron pillar, and he leaned against it, rubbing his skinned elbow and trying to catch his breath. Above his head the traffic rumbled back and forth across the bridge.

There was a dull thud on the other side of the bridge, followed by a second. Then footsteps crunching toward him over the gravel.

"Man, I'm over here," he called in a hoarse whisper.

"Who is that?"

"Muskrat."

"It's black as hell." It was a breathless voice in the darkness.

"Man, look out for them girders. I like to broke my arm. That you, Hector?"

"Yeah. Gyp's with me."

There was another dull thud on the side where Muskrat had picked himself up.

"Over here," called Muskrat in a low voice. "Who's that?"

"Me, Lipper." He was stumbling around, his footsteps sliding on the gravel. "I can't see my hand in front of my face."

"Man, watch out for them girders."

Hector was leading Gyp by the hand, one arm groping out in front of him. "Where are you?"

"Here, man," whispered Muskrat. "Grab hold here."

Hector reached around, found Muskrat's out-stretched hand, grasped it, and stopped.

"Whata run!" he said, breathing heavily. He let go of Gyp and pulled out his handkerchief and started mopping his face. Gyp dropped to the ground, panting, his head falling between his knees.

"I thought my lungs was gonna bust," he choked. "I'm dying for something to drink."

"Wait'll Marrie gets here and we'll hightail it to the Redeye," said Muskrat.

"Where are you guys?" called Lipper.

"Over here, man." Muskrat reached out and took the stumbling Lipper by the shoulders, pulling him over to them.

"Where's Marrie?"

"I don't know," said Lipper. He felt around gingerly for the iron pillar, his fingers finally catching hold of it. He propped himself against it. "Boy, I'm bushed!"

"Ten blocks is some run," said Gyp, breathing easier.

"But where the hell's Marrie? He's got the cash, man."

"How much you think we got?" said Hector, stuffing his handkerchief back into his pocket.

"Man, I don't care. We can worry about that at the Redeye. We oughta be getting out of here."

The traffic slackened on the bridge. The shuddering structure was quiet. Each of them tensed, glancing up, each straining his ears in the darkness.

"Ain't nothing," said Muskrat, after a moment. They relaxed, looking around, waiting. Hector started to light a cigaret and Muskrat knocked the match out of his hand.

"Cut that out," he snapped. "That's the trouble with us: we get careless. Man, you oughta be more careful, tripping a bell like that!" he said, turning on Gyp.

There was a light thump on the other side of the bridge. They all stared in that direction, listening.

"Marrie?"

"You know it," came a voice. They heard his footsteps running over the gravel.

"Man, don't bust your head on one of them steel beams!"

"I got eyes like a cat," he called. "I dance around them." He came up to them, laughing and breathless, pushing the mop of curls from his forehead.

The traffic picked up on the bridge. It began to shake and rattle.

"Man, what in the name of God took you so long?"

"I stopped to do some window shopping," he said, gasping for breath. He scratched a match on the pillar and with his other hand pulled from his shirtfront a long string of glistening stones. He waved the necklace in front of them, the stones sparkling in the matchlight.

"Wowie!"

"Boy! Diamonds?" said Gyp, pulling himself up and reaching out to touch the necklace.

"We're all here," said Muskrat, impatiently. "Let's tail ass."

"Wait'll I get my wind," said Marrie, forking the match between his fingers and thrusting out that arm to support himself against the pillar. "Uh-uh, mustn't touch, Gyp." He whipped the necklace away from Gyp's fingers and dropped it back into his shirtfront.

"Where'd you get them diamonds?" said Lipper.

"Man, let's get outa here!" cried Muskrat.

"Hey, what's the matter with your hand?" said Hector.

"Nothing," said Marrie, quickly shaking the hand that held the match. The hand was wrapped in a blood-soaked handkerchief. They all stared at it for a second.

"I smashed Coplin's window with my fist," he laughed. He pulled out a cigaret, lit it, then shook the match again and it went out.

"Nice going, Marrie!" cried Lipper.

"Could we *please* get outa here?" said Muskrat, flipping his cap around backwards.

"Anybody following?" Hector asked.

"I dodged them," said Marrie, laughing. He cocked his head to one side and spit a couple of flecks of tobacco off the tip of his tongue. "They're coming this way. Twenty miles an hour. We got a minute."

"They *can* step on the gas, you know," snarled Muskrat.

"You got the loot?" said Gyp.

"No, I tossed it down a sewer on the way." He leaned down and mussed Gyp's hair with his good hand. "Ole one track mind, you Gyp."

"No, but I mean . . ."

"You think I'll lose it after all the trouble we went to?" Marrie patted his bulging pocket, blowing a puff of smoke over one shoulder.

"Oh boy, oh boy!" squealed Lipper, rubbing his hands together.

"No chance of it getting away from me," continued Marrie. "I got a zipper put in now, you know." He unzipped and zipped the side pocket of his trousers a couple of times to show them.

"For christsakes, man, you're just too cool for me sometimes!" said Muskrat, turning away angrily. "Come on, cut that gab and let's get outa here!"

"Yeah, come on," said Lipper, pulling at Marrie.

"Okay, okay. Indian file. Alley-oop!" He swung away from the pillar and leaped out from beneath the bridge, heading down into the freightyard. The others followed, jogging after him.

"Give her the gas, boys!" he shouted, tossing back his head and breaking into a run. The others quickened their speed, jerking their heads back, and running faster, seeing the police car stopped on the bridge, the spotlight, hitched on the side, making short sweeps at the base of the bridge.

"Another minute and we'd've been dead ducks!" panted Muskrat, running up alongside Marrie. "Man, you're gonna be just a bit too casual one of these days."

Marrie threw back his head, opening his mouth wide and laughing. He reached across and gave Muskrat a light punch on the arm.

"You just mind what I say!" snapped Muskrat.

They crossed over the rows of railroad tracks, skirting the floodlights lining one side of the yard.

"Keep outa the light!" shouted Marrie, over his

shoulder. "The sign isn't on yet! Head for the heap!"

A hill of coal loomed up in the darkness. They scrambled up it, going down on their hands and knees and digging in with their fingers to make the steep climb. They ran over the top, crouching low on the other side. They could see the flashlights playing around the bottom of the bridge, and the police car on the bridge, its searchlight shooting an unmoving shaft of light down the tracks, its red blinker revolving nervously on top.

"You think maybe they'll come this way?" said Hector, wiping the sweat from his face with his handkerchief.

"Man, don't you worry. Them fatass cops don't go nowhere a car don't go."

"You never can tell." Hector handed the handkerchief over to Gyp, who was lying sprawled on the coal, and Gyp wiped his face.

"Well, man, if they come: dig in, dig in." Muskrat kicked at the coal. "You'll come out looking like a nigger, but, take it from me, it's better'n spending many a black night at Jamesburg."

They kept looking over toward the bridge. The flashlights were playing on the other side now. They all swung their heads around, hearing a sudden noise of coal sliding and clicking close by, of footsteps digging in, then silence.

"Who's there?"

"Bless me," came a cracked voice from near the bottom of the heap. "It's just a poor old woman out for a bit of coke to warm her bones."

"Friend or foe!" called Marrie, shoving his curls back from his eyes and peering down to where the voice came from.

"Hey, shutup, you dope!" whispered Hector, excitedly. "You don't know who it is!"

Someone was scrambling up the coal heap, moving toward them.

"I know who it is," said Lipper, raising himself on his knees. "It's Ashcan Annie, the crackpot millionaire!"

"Ay, it's you little blygarts!" croaked a woman's voice. She struggled up to them, panting and wheezing, and stooped down, leaning on one arm to catch her wind. Her bucket clanked on the coal beside her. "What've you rascals been up to?"

"Same thing you've been up to, ole girl," said Marrie, laughing, and taking her by the arm to steady her.

"Help an old lady, for Godsakes!" Her hand reached out in the darkness.

"Go on, go peddle your coal," said Hector.

"Come on, be good boys. Split something with a poor old lady." She blew her nose on the sleeve of her army coat and stretched out her fingers to them again.

Marrie unzipped his pocket and brought out a fistful of crumpled bills.

"Sorry, Annie, dear, can't see what it is," he said, pulling one out of the wad and handing it to her.

"Hey, man, what'n the hell you doing?" said Muskrat, getting up.

"That's a good boy," giggled Annie, tearing the bill from his hand. She lifted it to her mouth and ran her tongue over it. "Ill say a prayer for you," she said.

"Here, say two!" he laughed, peeling off a second bill and holding it out to her.

"Well, just take a look at Mr. Biggety," said

Muskrat, plonking his hands on his hips and spitting furiously to one side.

"An angel! A very angel!" squealed Annie, first smacking the bill with her lips, then snatching up Marrie's hand and kissing it. "I'll count a rosary for you, I will!"

"You do that, darling," said Marrie.

She stuffed both bills in the big pocket of her overcoat.

"Hey, man," said Muskrat, tapping Marrie on the shoulder. "That's *our* money too, remember?"

"Don't worry," laughed Marrie. "I'll subtract it from my cut."

"But, man, you can't see the size of them bills you're passing out so bighearted there," persisted Muskrat.

"Yeah, gee whiz," said Gyp, scraping his heel over the coal.

Annie darted looks from one to the other, then took the bills out of her pocket and stuffed them in her mouth, popping her lips tight over them.

"Aw, you guys worry too much," said Marrie, placing his hands on Muskrat's shoulders.

"Still and all, man, you get entirely too high and mighty . . ."

At that instant the light on the billboard behind the coalmound went on, illuminating ANSONIA BLUE COAL, in big letters.

There was a screech of whistles from the bridge; the policemen were leaning over the railing, waving their flashlights in the direction of the heap. They scattered. Annie picked up her coal bucket and, clutching it tightly under one arm, started running down the heap, the tails of her army coat spreading and flying behind her. She hurried over the railroad tracks, jumped a coupling, and disappeared behind the freightcars.

Once off the coal hill, the boys ran behind the floodlights, keeping in the shadows of the empty cars off on the siding.

"Whata we gotta run so fast for?" panted Muskrat, following close on the heels of Marrie.

"I don't wanta take them kind of chances!" Marrie shouted back.

When they got out of the freightyard they slowed down to a trot, looking back now and then. The police car was gone, the headlights of a couple of cars moved slowly over the bridge.

"Man, I'm plain pooped! We're plenty safe now," said Muskrat, pulling at Marrie's shirt and making him stop. Gyp came panting up to them from behind, and they moved up to the tracks and walked along over the ties, sweating and out of breath.

"Sure warms you up, don't it?" laughed Marrie.

"I shoulda been a trackrunner," said Gyp. "Maybe I'll look into that one of these days."

"Hey, Marrie, what's the big idea giving Ashcan Annie that money?" said Hector. "You must be nuts."

"Yeah," said Lipper. "Don't you know she's got thousands stashed away under her mattress?"

"Aw, go on. Don't believe everything you hear."

"But, man, my point is," said Muskrat, pulling up beside Marrie, "they mighta been tens, or even twenties, you gave off like it was air to that ole hag. Man, *our* money, that's the point!"

"Aw, Muskrat, you're too scroogey," laughed Marrie, yanking Muskrat's baseball cap off his head and pitching it over the side of the track. The others laughed. Muskrat raced off in the dark and came back, jamming the cap over his ears. "I'm serious!" he said, punching Marrie hard on the arm. "You're just too generous with what don't belong to you. And here's another lovetap for tossing my lid." He hauled off and cracked Marrie on the muscle.

"Ow! Ow!" cried Marrie, prancing away and rubbing his arm. "You guys, really . . ."

"When you sell that necklace, now you just cut it with the rest of us," said Muskrat, thrusting his hands deep in his back pockets and kicking at the ties.

"Yeah," said Lipper.

"So okay," said Marrie, spinning around to face them. He spread his arms, "Peace on earth," he said softly, lifting his face to the stars. "For godamighty's sake, lay off bugging me, will you?"

"Well, just you remember that cut," snorted Muskrat.

"Yeah," said Lipper.

About a quarter of a mile down the track the red neon sign of a bar glowed in the darkness. They began to walk faster, and as they got closer the words REDEYE BAR & GRILLE burned brightly in the plateglass windows on either side of the curtained door.

"Home, boys. Home to papa!" said Marrie, skipping down off the track. They jumped down the embankment and trotted toward the place. Muskrat pushed open the door and they walked singlefile into the bar.

"Ho, the riverrats!" shouted Wally, waving from behind the bar.

"Good evening, Parson Wallace!"

They waved to him, shouting and horseplaying as they trooped in the door.

"Give us a 'redeye special'!"

"Hi, Miss Pepper!"

As each of the boys walked by he rumpled Miss Pepper's hair.

"Lay off the coif, will you?" Miss Pepper reached back with his right hand and patted his hair into place. They leaned on the bar, huddling close to Miss Pepper.

"Whose coalbin you boys been in?" said Miss Pepper, nervously fingering one of the three lacquered curls plastered over his forehead. He did not look at them, but kept looking anxiously toward the window up front.

"Man, I never did go that coalheap idea!" said Muskrat, jumping up and down to get a glimpse of himself in the mirror behind the bar. "Just look at my black streaky face!"

They looked around at each other and burst out laughing.

"All I need's a headlamp!" shouted Muskrat.

"A bath'd be more like it," said Miss Pepper, pulling a pack of cigarets from the sleeve of his T-shirt and lighting one.

"Something looks funny," said Wally, coming down and leaning across the bar and looking at them. He motioned with his thumb toward the door in the rear. "Get moving."

"Aw, Wally . . ."

"Man, it's cold back there."

"You heard what I said. Get moving. There's none of you of age. It don't look good."

"How 'bout Marrie?" said Hector, pulling a long face and jerking his thumb toward Marrie.

"Him too. Hey, Marrie!" Wally said. "Go on, get back there with the rest of them."

"In a minute." Marrie was leaning on Miss Pepper's shoulders. Wally waved his arm at the others, and they turned, slouching and looking back at Marrie, grumbling, as they plodded into the backroom.

"Come on. You too, pretty boy!" Wally repeated.

"Just a minute, Wally. Take it easy." Marrie leaned down and kissed Miss Pepper on the neck.

"Okay, handsome, with the others," said Wally, motioning toward the backroom.

"Ah, but, Wally, aren't you gonna give me a little time to make out with my baby?" he said, sliding onto a stool next to Miss Pepper and putting his arms around his waist.

"Baby nothing. Keep your crummy hands offa me," said Miss Pepper, drawing away.

"Ah, now, baby," said Marrie, holding his hands out in front of him. "Well, I guess you're right at that."

"Come on, get back there," said Wally, pouring whiskey into a glass. "I'm not gonna tell you again."

"But, Wally, we shook them," he said, turning and hanging on the bar.

"Shookum-schmookum. Get back there. You're not twenty-one yet, remember."

"It stinks back there. And it's cold. Let me stay here with my baby."

"Get your black mitts off me!" snapped Miss Pepper.

Marrie brought the necklace out of his shirt, untangled it and slipped it around Miss Pepper's neck, clasping it from behind.

"For the love of God!" Miss Pepper gasped, bending his head and looking down at the stones glistening on his chest. He turned his head to Marrie, amazed.

"You're my boy," said Marrie, laying his hand on Miss Pepper's shoulder.

Wally lifted the wooden flap and came out from behind the bar. Marrie was bending over Miss Pepper and Wally took him by the scruff of the neck and the seat of the trousers and hurried him toward the backroom.

"Okay, okay, I'm going," cried Marrie. "Let me go, will you!"

Wally pushed him toward the door and stood, hands on hips, watching until Marrie opened the door and went in. Muskrat stuck his head out.

"Shut that door! I'll be back with you guys in a minute."

Muskrat thumbed his nose at Wally and quickly kicked the door shut with his foot.

Wally walked back to the bar, ducking beneath the wooden flap, and went up to wait on three sailors who had just come in. A tall thin Negro had followed the sailors in the door. He went over to the piano, leaned one elbow on the top and stood eyeing the sailors up and down.

Then he walked to the end of the bar, gazing over his shoulder at them.

"Why, Miz Peppah! As I live and breathe!" he exclaimed, extending his hand palm down to be kissed. "I do declare! It's been ever so long!"

"You're off your beat, aren't you, Rosemary?" Miss Pepper ignored the hand and crunched out his cigaret in the ashtray. He promptly lit another and continued staring toward the other end of the bar, where the three sailors had seated themselves.

"Don't scold-la-belly-roll, Miz Peppah. See, I

brought the fleet in," he giggled, flipping his fingers toward the front.

"That was very thoughtful of you," said Miss Pepper. "What else is in the wind?"

Rosemary perched on the stool next to him, primly crossing his legs and leaning his elbows on the bar. "Nothing but air, air, air," he sighed.

"Well, how's business in the Black Bottom?"

"Nil," sighed Rosemary. "Positively nili-ili-ili-o. Oh, Wally, do be a dolly and draw me a bourbon." Rosemary loosened the purple mesh scarf from around his throat.

"Well, if you can afford high liquor," said Miss Pepper, blowing smoke through his nostrils. "Or do you work for the house?"

"Tut, tut. No jealousy, Miz Peppah."

Wally set the drink down in front of Rosemary. "How're the boys?"

"Lousy."

"Miz Peppah's got the complaints, the laments, and God knows what all," said Rosemary, lifting the glass and taking a dainty sip. "Won't ever be friendly with his old pal."

Wally lifted a glass of whiskey onto the counter and set it in Miss Pepper's hands.

"What's eating you? Go start a dart game with the sailboys."

"I'm sick to the hilt of playing darts." Miss Pepper took out a small mascara kit, dabbed the tiny brush in it and, looking into his compact mirror, began reblacking his lashes.

"I'm positively winded," said Rosemary. "For sea legs them sailboys don't do bad. It was all I could do to keep up with them. Ten block-a-locks, imagine!"

"Steering the trade my way," laughed Wally. "That's a nice boy."

"Well, I'm always thinking of you, baby. Whenever I see a uniform I always think to myself, Wally—uh-huh—Wally."

"I'll bet you do."

"Hey-o-ley, where'd you get the icecubes?" said Rosemary, gazing popeyed at the necklace around Miss Pepper's neck. He leaned over and examined the stones carefully.

"Marrie gave them to me," Miss Pepper said, importantly. "I guess he busted a window. He came in with his hand wrapped up."

"Oh, are the dear boys here?" said Rosemary, darting his head in every direction.

"I put them in the backroom," Wally said. "I don't want them out front."

"I wish somebody'd bust a window for me," said Rosemary.

Miss Pepper smeared a little rouge on his cheeks.

"That's right, baby, you spruce up."

Wally ambled down to where the sailors were. "Why don't you boys play a game of darts? No, wait. I'll set you up to a couple beers on the house."

"That's mighty white of you, mister." The three sailors settled themselves at the bar.

Wally drew the beers and set them in front of the sailors.

He started to turn but one of the sailors, lean-faced, reached over and grabbed him by the arm.

"Much obliged for the beers, mate."

"That's okay."

Wally turned to go again, but the sailor kept hold of his arm. Wally swung around.

"Hey, tell me, mate, who's the dame sitting down there?" he said, grinning.

"You mean, Miss Pepper?" Wally propped one leg on a shelf and glanced down to where the sailor was pointing.

"Is that her name?"

"Say, she's some dish," said the second sailor, bearded.

"Yeah, she's been giving us the eye ever since we came in," said the third, a redhead. He nudged up close to Wally. "Is that nigger her boyfriend?"

"Yeah, does he pimp for her?" said the leanfaced sailor. "We seen him downtown."

"That's a hot one!" said Wally, slapping his thigh and bursting out laughing. "No, the colored boy's Rosemary."

"Rosemary? Hey, is that his real name?"

"Yeah."

"No kidding."

"Both very nice boys," said Wally. "Like an introduction?"

"Boys, you say?" said the redhead. "You mean the other one, too? . . . What's 'er name . . .?"

"Miss Pepper," said Wally.

"You coulda fooled me," said the leanfaced sailor.

"Hey, what kinda place is this anyhow?"

"Yeah," said the redhead. "Girls that turn out to be boys. Whatta you got in the backroom?"

"Look," said Wally, spreading his arms on the bar and leaning toward them, "Anybody can come here and have a drink or play darts or anything, so long as he minds his own business and behaves hisself. It's my place," he said, tapping his fingers on his chest. "I run it to suit me."

"We got you, keepie. Don't get sore."

"I just want you to understand that. That's all."

"We understand."

"Hey, matie," said the leanfaced one, leaning confidential-like over the bar. "Where're the women?"

"Yeah, buddie," said the redhead. "That's all we wanta know. None of that joyboy stuff for us."

"Stick around," said Wally. "They come in now and then."

He turned to go.

"No hard feelings, matie."

"I'm not sore," Wally said. "Enjoy yourselves. Call me if you want anything."

He walked to the other end of the bar.

"What's with the sailboys?" said Miss Pepper, lighting another cigaret.

"No dice."

"You think so," said Miss Pepper, staring hard at the three sailors.

"Don't get miffled," giggled Rosemary. "Just make use of your God-given patience, honey."

"Excuse me," said Wally. "I forgot something."

He lifted the flap, walked back to the rear and opened the door. The room was full of cigaret smoke. Muskrat, Lipper and Hector were sprawled on the beerkegs. Gyp sat hunched in a corner, his arms resting on his knees, his head rolling from side to side. He was asleep. Marrie stood looking out the window, impatiently flicking the ash from a cigaret. He swung around as Wally entered.

"Well, well, at long last!" he smiled, blowing a jet of smoke toward the ceiling.

"Man, I thought you forgot all about us," said Muskrat, pushing his baseball cap back and sitting up, rubbing his eyes.

"I was busy." He walked over and kicked at Gyp's shoes. "Hey, Bozo, wake up."

"What? What?" Gyp's head jerked up. He looked around with heavy eyes.

"Okay," said Wally, walking to the center of the room and lighting a cigaret. "Now that we're all awake and present, what was the good deed for the day?"

"Pilsky's store . . . ninety-six bucks," said Marrie.

"Chicken feed," sneered Wally, resting his foot up on a keg and eyeing them.

"Get outa here, man!"

"Listen, we mighta had more'n that, only we come across Ashcan Annie and big-hearted Ben here," Hector poked his thumb in Marrie's ribs—"hada go and give her a couple of bills."

"Yeah," said Muskrat, slipping off the barrel and walking over to Wally, his thumbs hitched in his pockets. "And it was so dark we couldn't see how much they were. Mighta been a hundred dollars for all we know."

"Fat chance," laughed Marrie, drawing his legs up on a keg and hugging his knees. "I'm nuts about them women."

"You're just plain nuts, buster," said Gyp, getting up and stretching and yawning.

"I'm telling you, man, you get too high-and-mighty with other people's money."

Marrie exploded in laughter.

"You should talk!" he howled.

"Where'd you meet Annie?" Wally said.

"On the coal heap, after we jumped the bridge," said Hector. "She was swiping coal in a bucket."

"Well, how was the shopping trip at Pilsky's?" said Wally, rubbing his chin.

"Not a hitch," said Marrie. "The two of them stayed outside on watch, while me and Muskrat and Gyp broke inside."

"Man, Gyp, you're staying outside next time," said Muskrat. "Gyp hada go and trip the burglar alarm," he said to Wally. "Otherwise they wouldn't a never knowed nothing."

"What?" said Wally, stepping forward.

"Lay off, will you?" Gyp said, "We all goof once in a life."

"Did they see where you was heading?" persisted Wally.

"Naw," said Hector. "They chased us to the bridge. We gave them the buzz in the coal pile."

"Marrie mighta got us caught," said Lipper. "He took time to swipe a necklace."

"But we ducked them, didn't we?" said Marrie, turning on Lipper."

"Even so . . ."

"Man, show Wally that pretty necklace," said Muskrat. "We all get a cut since he was so free and easy with our dough," he explained to Wally.

"I don't wanta look at no necklace now," said Wally, glancing sharply at Marrie. "Let me take a look at that hand."

"It's nothing," said Marrie, stuffing the hand in his pocket and moving away.

"I'll get some iodine and something clean to wrap it in," Wally said.

"Suit yourself." Marrie shuffled over to the window and stared out into the darkness.

"You oughtn't to keep it dirty like that," Wally said. "A cut . . ."

"It's okay, goddamn it!" snapped Marrie, his face coloring. He pushed the mop of curls back from his forehead and continued staring out the window.

Wally looked at him for a second, then turned to the others.

"What're you boys gonna do with all that money?"

"Spend it. What the hell you think?" said Hector.

"Send Miss Pepper back here," said Marrie.

"No, I ain't gonna send Miss Pepper back here."

"What the hell's the matter?"

"I'm not gonna have any more teajags on my hands, that's all. It's enough having you winedrunk or whatever without your goofing off on them crazy cigarets."

"I guess it's our money!" snapped Marrie.

"And I guess I'm the boss here! Maybe you think different?"

Marrie started to say something, but kept quiet, glaring defiantly at his reflection in the glass.

Wally stared around at the others, hands on hips. Each cast his eyes down and was silent.

He lifted his leg off the barrel and walked over to the window.

"You divvy the money up?"

"Yeah." Marrie reached into his pocket. "Here. We thought maybe you should get a cut this time."

Wally shoved the money away. He walked over to the door. "What you all want to drink?"

There were shufflings of one foot to the other, they looked uneasily at each other.

"Well, come on, come on," said Wally, coaxing with his fingers.

"Whiskey," said Gyp, punching a keg.

"Okay."

"Me too," said Marrie.

"Beer for me," said Muskrat.

"Beer?" said Wally, pointing two fingers at Hector and Lipper. They both nodded.

"All right. Now look, you guys. When you have your fill I want you to skidaddle. No roughhousing back here. And no hanging around. I don't want nobody to find you here. You get me?"

"Man, it's cold as a witch's behind outside," said Muskrat, shrugging his shoulders and shivering.

"Just do as I say, that's all. Go somewhere. But no going downtown and thinking you're all don juans with the tail. You nearly got picked up last time. You understand?"

"Man, you're getting as bad as a warden."

"You can all rot in Jamesburg. You think I care? I don't care."

He turned and stepped out, shutting the door behind him.

The bar was warm and smoky, full of low talk. A couple more customers had come in and Rosemary had waited on them. Wally nodded to the newcomers and went behind the bar. As he started to fix the drinks, the front door opened and two policemen stepped in. One of the customers quickly emptied his glass and, pulling his hat low over his eyes, slipped out the sidedoor.

One policeman stood by the door. The other walked up to the bar, leaning on it, and motioned to Wally.

"Like to have a look in your backroom, Wally boy," he said.

"Help yourself." Wally went back to the tap, took the drinks he had poured and set them up before the customers on the counter.

"A little something on the house," he said.

"Saved by the cop-o-lop-olos!" giggled Rosemary, taking the drink.

The policeman stopped by Miss Pepper, tweaking him on the shoulder.

"It's not your tree, buster. Go pinch your apples somewhere else."

He leaned over, "You'll be sorry one of these

days," said the policeman, grinning and patting his nightstick.

"Can't be any more sorrier than I am," Miss Pepper said. "Shove off."

The policeman stared at the necklace for a moment.

"Them're a nice set of rocks," he said. "Where'd you get them?"

"They're a wedding present from a dead husband."

"Watch your brains!" He poked Miss Pepper between the legs, then danced away, smiling.

"Watch it, blueboy. You coppers think you can get everything for nothing."

"Why, Pepper gal," said the policeman, resting his hand on Miss Pepper's shoulder, "I swear you're getting hair on your chest."

"Take your clammy claw off me, blueboy."

Rosemary reached out and pinched the policeman on the cheek.

"How's my baby?" he said, rolling his dark eyes.

"This ain't Ash Wednesday," snarled the policeman, rubbing his cheek with the back of his hand. "You'd be lynched for that, south of Washington, my friend."

"Just hang me, blueboy, on a sour apple treede-leedeleedel . . ."

"Hey, mastermind," called Wally, from the rear of the room. "You coming to inspect this backroom or not?"

"Take it easy," the policeman shouted. He turned, squinting his eyes at Rosemary. "Just don't you think I wouldn't hang you on any tree, nigger. You watch how flip I'll let you get with me."

"Hmph! Big badge, big stickelickilo!" Rosemary

snorted, and swung around to the bar, picking up his drink.

Miss Pepper was still looking in the direction of the three sailors, who were now standing and watching intently the trio at the other end of the bar.

The policeman looked Rosemary up and down, then walked back to where Wally was waiting.

Wally pushed the door open, stepping aside to let the policeman go in first. The room was cold and empty. Wally took a quick look around the bar, then closed the door after him.

"Kind of chilly in here," said the policeman, briskly rubbing his hands together and nodding toward the open window.

"I always keep the window open," said Wally. "Stinks in here. Sour beer. You know. I'll close it if it bothers you."

"No, it don't bother me," said the policeman. He sat down on a beerkeg, throwing one leg over the other and grinning up at Wally.

"I'll shut it anyway," said Wally. He went over and closed the window. "It don't stink so bad now." He came back, jamming his hands in his back pockets, and stood in front of the policeman. "I don't know what to do," he said. "I tried everything. You know them little perfumed things you hook inside your toilet? I strung them all around in here. Don't work. Worse than before. Makes the place smell like a cathouse." He kicked at one of the barrels.

"Really?" The policeman pulled out a pair of leather gloves and began lightly slapping one on the other. "You should write that stuff down. You'd make a million."

"You think so, huh?"

The policeman coughed up some phlegm and spit

between his legs, rubbing it out with the heel of his shoe. "You got a cellar?" he said, glancing up and wiping his mouth with the back of his hand.

"No, I ain't got a cellar. Why?"

"Was just wondering. Most places got a cellar for this stuff," he said, whacking one of the kegs with his leather gloves.

"No, there's no cellar in this place. Makes it damp as hell in winter, you know."

"I can imagine," said the policeman, smiling at him. "I never thought to ask you before if you had a cellar or not."

Wally walked over to the window and looked out.

"I noticed you wasn't in too much of a hurry to get back here."

The policeman continued to smile.

"Okay," he said. "How about it?"

Wally reached into his pocket, brought out a brown envelope and tossed it to the policeman. The policeman caught it, tore it open and pulled out the bill inside. He smoothed it out on his palm and went over and held it beneath the light.

"This all?"

"What the hell more do you want?"

"Don't get sore, Wallyboy." He pushed the bill in his pocket, then crumpled up the envelope and threw it behind the kegs. "There's no little package goods to go, maybe?"

Wally shrugged his shoulders, turning again to the window.

"Aw, come off it, Wallyboy."

"How 'bout a fifth of my blood for a chaser?" he said, swinging around to face the policeman. "You got an empty bottle?"

"Temper, temper, Wallyboy." The policeman

chuckled and tapped Wally lightly on the arm with his leather gloves. Wally looked at him a second.

"Wait here," he said.

He went into the bar and came back a minute later carrying a bulging brown paper bag, twisted at the top. He shut the door and handed the bag to the policeman.

"See you," he said, staring down at the floor.

"That's the sport," said the policeman, unbuttoning his coat and thrusting the bag inside. "Gets mighty cold these nights. You should know. No cellar or nothing."

"Okay, okay," said Wally, impatiently. "I got business to attend to. My customers are deserting me."

"I'll take my exit here," said the policeman, stepping over to the window. "It seems pretty convenient." He slid the window up, stooped, and swung one leg over the sill. "Goodnight, Wally-boy. Take it easy." He started to lift the other leg over, but paused. "Oh, by the way," he said, snapping his fingers, "tell your boys to take it easy. I might have to run them in one of these days if things get any hotter. Irregardless."

He waved his hand, smiling, ducked out and was gone.

"You go pound sand, you goddamned leech!" Wally went over and slammed the window shut. "Crusty bastards," he muttered. He flipped out the light and stepped outside, banging the door after him.

The bar was silent and empty, hazy with smoke. All had gone.

A train went thundering by, shaking the building. The windows rattled. Wally glanced up at the clock, waited til the train had passed, then swung around and went to the front door. He opened the door and looked around outside in the darkness. All was still. He slammed the door and locked it. There was the sharp blast of an engine whistle down in the freightyard. He stood listening til the sound had died away, then flipped the switch, turning off the red neon signs in the windows, and turned out the other lights, leaving a small one burning in the rear.

The Desert

Two men sat slumped against the wall of the adobe hut, their broad-brimmed hats tilted low over their eyes, their hands resting quietly on their kneecaps. Each pair of eyes, aslant, watched without expression from their corners a man, a black speck in the distance, approaching over the desert.

A third man, short and fat, with a bandana, black from wear, stretched over his skull and knotted at his throat, squatted before a fire a few paces from the door of the hut. On a tripod of sticks knotted together at the top with a leather throng, hung a pot in which bubbled beans and chunks of bacon. In the pot was a wooden paddle which he now and then took in his hand and turned idly, stirring the beans. He was also watching the approach of the stranger.

A blanket hung over the door of the hut and each of the rough-cut windows was covered with sheets of newspaper, brown and crumbling from the sun. At one corner of the building was a large cactus plant on the prongs of which hung a shirt and a pair of dungarees. In the bed of an arroyo, sloping down a few yards from the hut, sat an old open touring car, highbacked and rusting. In the shade of the car a dog lay on its side, as if it were dead. Silt drifted in a fine heap against its curled spine. Occasionally the dog flicked its rag of a tail, striking at flies gnawing raw patches in its flanks.

The sun beat down with a dry, white glare over the desert. Far off, the tablerock pressed hazy and pink against the horizon. There was no sound, no wind.

The man in the distance rose and fell from view as he climbed one drift of sand and then plunged down out of sight before ascending the next. The man seated before the fire waited until the man got to a crest, watched him intently, and when he disappeared again between drifts, turned his attention to the small cloud of insects hovering over the cookpot. He brushed them away, lazily, with his plump dark arm.

"Off the track. Lost," he said.

"Thirsty and hungry. Maybe loco from the heat. Maybe an escaped convict," said one of the men crouched against the wall, Hook, a thin, fine-boned man, with a sharp nose and his legs thin as a bird's in his tight levis. On his boots were silver spurs, highly polished, sparkling in the sun.

"Last one was kinda pretty," said Mex, the man at the fire.

"Black suit—that ain't no prison suit." Capon was a thick man, his heavy arms folded across his chest, his hands tucked beneath his armpits.

"Black sucks up the sun," said Mex.

"Never can tell," Capon went on. "Hope not another one of them joyrides in Theodora: 'Turn this way, turn that, who zat following us?' And the desert as flat as your granny's tit and not a human soul for miles and all the while the gun butt in the nape of your neck. I hope he's something different this time."

"It'll break the day," said Hook. "I'm glad for that. And if he's got a gun, I don't care."

"Man wants a little something new to make his heart beat," said Mex.

They watched closely now as the man became more distinct, the two against the wall shifting their bodies slightly to see better. The man wore a dark suit and on his head was a wide-brimmed black hat which he occasionally lifted and fanned his face with. Now and again he cast quick glances behind him as he hurried on, in long-legged strides, stumbling and sliding over the sand.

"A loose-tongued preacher," said Hook. "Nits of God in his hair and the lice of the devil crapping over his skull."

"Two-bits he's a undertaker."

"One of them bone-frillers?" said Mex. "Angel smile on his face while one hand or the other gooses your wallet every time you turn to blow your nose for the departed? Well, for myself, I hope he's not."

"Whatever he is, I wish he'd hurry up and get here."

Now the stranger was out of the drifts and walking over the flat ground surrounding the hut. He had a handkerchief tied around his neck and he kept glancing from side to side and then at the men, walking quickly, his long arms swinging.

Hook pinched between his leathery fingers a twist of paper into which he carefully spilled grains of tobacco from a small cotton sack. Capon rolled his back, scratching it against the adobe wall. Flakes of dried clay fell down in a little heap where his buttocks rested.

"Howdy," said Mex. He got up, rubbing his hands slowly up and down his hips, and smiled at the newcomer. "We been watching you."

The other two rose from their crouched position and eyed him.

The stranger stood near the corner of the hut, his hat in his hands and his fingers snapping and unsnapping the brim. His eyes darted from one to the other while a shy smile contorted his mouth. He stood heels close together, playing with his hat, his throat working. His face was flushed from the heat and there were rings of grime around his neck and in the creases of his brow. Tall, with long bony fingers, and legs that were shaking a little—his hair hanging down over his ears, creased about the skull from his hatband.

"Where you heading, strange?" said Hook, narrowing his eyes and puffing on the cigaret.

"This looks as good a place as any."

Hook squinted at him.

"You mean you ain't got no destination?"

"No," he stammered, looking and then not looking at them, at their hard-set faces. "Which way is California?"

"Out there," said Mex, pointing toward the horizon.

"I've never seen the Pacific." He put his hat on his head. "Nor orange trees."

The men laughed.

"See one wave you seen 'em all."

"Oranges're behind barbed wire," sneered Hook.

"I wouldn't want to pick them," said the stranger. "I don't believe what you say about the waves."

"Oh, like the sand riffs here, 'cepting out there they're wet."

"I'm William."

"We'll call you Reverend. Rev, for short," said Hook.

Mex went up and walked all around the stranger. The stranger stood still, his eyes following the man as he moved around him. Then Mex reached up and began touching the stranger's hair.

"Don't worry none, strange. He ain't seen clean hair in so long—nor none so soft."

"Say," snapped Capon suddenly, stalking over and pointing his finger in William's face. "You don't know where you're going and you don't know where you're at.—You ain't escaping, are you?"

William thrust his hands in his pockets and looked down at the ground.

"A goddamned convict!" cried Capon, advancing on him. "Where's your gun?" He started to beat the man's coat.

William pushed him away firmly with one hand. Capon stood staring at him, his arms swung wide from his sides, his fists doubled.

"You listen.—What I am—" said William, heatedly, smoothing his coat. "I'm a mistaken man.— Yes—I—"

He stared off over the land, his hands trembling.

"What was you saying?" said Hook, scraping his beard with his finger.

"Have you any water, please?"

"Get a dipper of water, Mex."

Mex went behind the hut.

"Queer talk you got in your mouth, strange."

"Sit down a spell, son," said Capon, coming forward and taking him by the elbow. "We got water."

"Thank you, kindly."

"Here, in the doorway," said Capon, leading him over, "where there's shade."

William sat down with a gasp and stretched his legs out before him. There were spots of red amidst spots of white in his face. He snatched his hat off and began beating it rapidly in front of him. The two men stood watching, curious and quiet. Mex, waddling, hurried from around the corner of the building, carefully balancing a ladleful of water. He handed it to the man and said, "Guess you're hungry too. We got beans."

William threw the water down in one gulp. "A bit more, please," he said, holding out the empty ladle.

Mex hustled off around to the back of the hut again.

"It's good to be with men," William said, hoarsely, leaning forward and clasping his fingers around his knees.

Hook flipped his cigaret into the fire.

"What you doing off the road, Rev?"

He looked up, thought a minute, and said, "There's something uneasy in me. It's like I'm all known now and nowhere to hide." He blushed and let his head fall.

Capon coughed and, turning away, spat in the dust. "You'll feel better after sundown," he said.

Mex came back with the water and handed it to William, then went over to the fire. He gave a last stir with the paddle, lifted it out and thumped it on the pot's edge, watching as the thick strings of blackstrap molasses fell back into the beans.

"Slop's done," he said.

" 'Bout time," said Capon, stretching his arms wide. "My belly's got the windjams, it's that empty." He slugged himself in the gut.

"Beans'll push it down a cave or two," said Hook, grinning and loosening his belt.

"I'll play you some after-dinner music," said Capon, slapping him on the back.

"A treat to my ears but it'll take me a clothespin to listen."

"We'll shoot perfume around, comes the bass parts. Jist for you, Hookie, darling."

"And that'll shoot me, that whiff of a woman."

"I guess you gotta strong wind in your belly, aintcha, Reverend?"

"I'm not very hungry."

"Well, a man needs to eat. And when he's et himself full, he starts thinking about a woman, and when he ain't got a woman—"

"He jist conks out to sleep," laughed Hook. "And dreams 'em up. So many quiff he can't handle 'em all. I wisht I had me jist *one* of them babes a' the hunnerds I dreamt. Um-*um!*" He ran his tongue around his mouth and strode over to the pot.

Mex came out of the hut carrying four clay bowls stacked in his hands.

"Hey, Mexicali, can't you stew us up a woman outa this mess someday?"

"I ain't no frigging witch. If you want a woman take ole Theodora into town for a grease job. Now get outa my way while I dish up the beans, nectar a' the gods and sweethard a' the eye o' men for miles around."

He ladled some beans into a bowl and handed them to William. "Guests first. Awful coarse, Reverend. We eat with our hands."

"Then I will." He went over to the hut with his bowl and sat down against the wall.

"Your fingers get calluses after a while," called Capon over his shoulder as he held his bowl out to Mex. "Beanheels, we call 'em. Careful you don't burn yourself."

The dog came wandering up from the arroyo, paused a moment to sniff the air, then loped straight to the fire.

"The only time Mange wakes up is chow time," said Mex. "Only sharp thing about that dog is his snoot can tell jist about when the beans is done to a turn."

The dog sniffed at the rim of the pot, then groaned pleadingly up into Mex's face, his tail whipping the sand.

"Quit kicking up dust, you'll get yours," he said, kneeing the animal aside. "Humans first."

Hook and Capon sat backs against the wall, blowing on their beans before picking them up to put into their mouths, and then licked the juice off their fingers.

Mex filled his own bowl and then threw a paddleful of beans on the sand. The dog jumped on them and lapped them up in one gulp.

"Mange'll get disaterry, all the time you're throwing his grub on the bare ground," said Hook. "All that dirt he eats stuck with it."

"Ain't killed him yet," said Mex, sending another pile of beans scudding in the sand. He came over and sat down in front of the men, balancing his bowl on one knee, and began to eat loudly with his fingers, sucking at the molasses as it ran down his wrists.

"Day's so hot," he said, "my armpits are panting."

"We smell them potent elbows," said Hook, running his tongue meticulously over his knuckles.

"We take sandbaths out here," said Mex to William. "Just like regular chickens. It's kinda undignified for a man, hunched nekkid and scratching and heaving dust on hisself, wouldn't you think? But it keeps the lice low."

"I told you to save up your water," said Capon,

smearing his fingers around the bottom of the bowl. "Figure it, a bladderful a day and come Saturday night you'd have a oil barrel full to take a bath in." He got up and went over and helped himself to more beans.

"D'ruther take a sandbath," said Mex. "And you oughtn't to talk that way before the Reverend."

"Don't mind me," said William, wiping his fingers on a crumpled handkerchief.

"You want more beans, Rev?"

"I'm not hungry."

"They're lousy but you get used to them," said Capon, striding back and sitting down with a fresh bowlful.

"I see you never pass them up," said Mex, carefully picking an insect out of his beans. He stared at it clinging to his fingernail, then blew it away.

The dog came up and sniffed at William's hands. He reached out to pet him but the dog backed away, his head to one side, looking at the stranger.

"He thinks you're from Mars," said Hook.

The dog's head swung sharply to its haunches where the gray bubble of a tick poked through the fur. He rubbed it with his nose and then muzzled into the fur, grasping the thing in his mouth and tore it from his flesh. He cracked the tick between his teeth and swallowed it.

"Ouch!" cried William.

"Why not?" said Mex, scooping beans into his mouth. "They eat him."

He tilted the bowl to his lips, draining the last of the juice, then set it aside and lay back on the sand, cupping his hands behind his head. Hook rolled and lit a cigaret and tipped his hat down low over his eyes, smoking. William looked from one to

the other, then out into the distance and back
again. He tied his handkerchief into one knot after
another.

The dog trotted back down the arroyo. With one
forepaw lifted, he looked from left to right, sniffing,
then scuttled under the car. Worming his body
around in the sand, hollowing it, he lay still and
went to sleep.

"Day like this," said Capon, unbuckling his belt
and letting his hands fall loosely at his sides,
" 'minds me of the time my granny lit the fire in the
oven to get it heated for her to bake a pie. Mean-
time, she goes out to get more kindling, comes back,
stacks it, crimples the crust-edge of the pie a little,
forks holes in the top, then sticks her nose in the
oven to smell how the heat was and, lord! what a
stench she gets.—Rears back.—Sticks her finger in
her jaw, asking, what can it be? So, pinching her
nose, she swings open the door wide and gapes in—
and, you'll never guess! You know what it was? Ole
Tearose, ancient aunt-gora cat she had all her life,
crawled in there to take a nap and got baked instead. Well, Granny has almost a stroke, you know.
—She got seven other cats but Tearose her special
pet—and the stink! Well, she draw a bucket from
the well and splash it on that fire fast as lightning—
but ole Tearose a gonner—hair singed to a frazzle
and I'd say from Gran's telling it, nearabout medi-
um-sized done—her tail (what was so plumey and
fine) coiled up tight as a rattler and her feet poked
straight out, no fur on 'em, jist like four burnt
matchsticks—and her eyes shot from her head like
busted grapes.—Pretty eyes she had too—weird—
one green, the other pink.—Well, what was ole
Granny gonna do?—The pie set there unbaked and

Tearose was, and the stench of her filling the kitch-
en enough to kill a man with leather lungs.—Well,
Gran throw open the windows and then she let
Tearose cool a bit 'fore she try to lift her out and,
lo, when she try to, that cat is melted to the grill
like baked cement.—And Gran, tears running down
her cheeks, she fetch Grampa's razor and, you know,
poor thing, only thing she could do, she sliced that
prize cat of hers off each and every one of them
grill bars.—Yessir.—Took a hour or more to do it.
—And when she got it done, she put what was left
of Tearose in a paper bag and buried her out back
of the hollyhocks.—She come back and she was so
upset and sad, she hadn't no heart to light that
oven again.—So what does she do but put on her
hat and trots down to Miz Huffington's to set and
have a cup of tea and collect herself.—And she tell
Huffie all 'bout it, and then she and Huffie have a
big cry together and they both feel better.—But
Granny didn't never forget.—And what every time
she lit the oven after that, Tearose would come back,
like a ghost you might say, every time smelling up
the room. But after a couple of months the stink of
her got all burnt out of the oven and Gran felt better for that, I can tell you. Why there wasn't a
breakfast or a dinner she'd cook and she wouldn't
bust into tears or start sniveling in the stew.—
And it got Grampa sore. 'A course he was still chew-
ing bile over that razor of his Gran had chipped
and wrecked all to hell that day, the one with a
motherapearl handle he had sent C O D special de-
livery from New York City."

Capon chuckled and flicked a fly off his nose.

"Being so ancient, she mighta died first.—You
know, crawled in there to die stead'a nap," said

Mex, "and was off into cat-limbo long before the heat got to her."

"I don't think Granny ever thought of that. Mighta cheered her up somewhat."

"More company," said Hook, nodding to the west. They turned and looked.

Across the sand a horse came plodding on which sat an Indian, wearing a 10-gallon hat, an onion sack bulging with cans of beer slung to the saddle-horn. The horse's head slunk almost to the ground, the reins trailing in the dust between its hoofs. The Indian sat swaying in the saddle, a can of beer pressed to his lips, his free hand gesticulating aim-lessly to the air.

The horse, without once lifting its head, green saliva foaming at its jaws, padded quietly up to the men and came to a halt.

"Howdy, Morning Light!" exclaimed Mex, going up, hand extended.

The Indian lifted a finger, circled it in the air, smiled foolishly and fell off the horse. He landed in a heap on the other side, still clutching the can from which beer dribbled into the earth.

Mex laid a hand against the horse's ribs, then, bending his knees, he peered under the animal's belly at the collapsed Indian and said, "Why, Morning Light, this is a helluva note. You come to pay us a call and here you are drunk enough for ten redskins."

"Glub," said Morning Light, crooking his finger at the sky. "More beer, Chester Axehead. I know you of old."

"He ain't no fun when he's this way," Capon said out of the corner of his mouth to William.

"He ain't killed no white man yet though when

he's been on a toot," said Hook, walking over to the horse. "He's a good Indian." He reached between the horse's front legs and picked up the reins.

"Good innien," muttered Morning Light, trying to pull himself up. "Don't eat jelly on my bread. Hair won't fall out—teeth won't fall out—like white man. Mexicali, give a good innien a hand here."

As Hook led the horse to the rear of the hut, Mex grabbed one arm and Capon came over and took the other and together they hauled the Indian to his feet.

"Obliged," he said thickly. "Sick a' looking at the sky."

The two men held him up as the Indian stood unsteadily on his feet, his head wobbling around, his eyes narrowed and blinking.

"Who zat? Unnertaker? Come to get my carcass. Worth a plug quarter."

"Why, that's a guest of ours," said Mex. "Reverend, this is Morning Light, old acquaintance."

"How do you do."

"Reverend, eh? Thought you was taker-under. Ooo, lay me in the shade."

They led him over to the adobe and propped him against the wall. He slid down hard in a sitting position and looked around.

"Hey, where's my horse? Who stole my horse? My beer, where's my beer?" he croaked, struggling to get to his feet. "String the bastard up. There's a law."

"Now that's no way to talk about a white man," said Mex, placing his hands on the Indian's shoulders and pushing him down. "Hook's taking your horse to water him. He'll bring you back your beer."

"Well, he better," grumbled the Indian, letting his head rock loosely against the wall. "There's a free lynch law in this territory 'bout horse-thieving."

"Yeah, fifty years ago," said Capon. "You been reading them Westerns again."

Hook came back carrying the onion sack in his hand.

"I don't know as you need more of this," he said, dropping the sack at the Indian's feet.

"Need beer like I need a bath. Bad." He burrowed his nose in his armpit. "Foo! Can't stand the stink of myself. Get drunk."

"Where'd you get dough for booze?" said Capon. "You ain't never had no cash before."

"Celebrate!" exclaimed the Indian. "Have beer. Star—me, a star."

"Some star," sneered Hook. "Can't even sit his horse right."

"Thinks he's a star," said Mex, rubbing his chin. "You hit your head when you fell?"

"Not star inna sky, idiot. Movie star! They shot pitcher out at Shadow Rock. I was extra brave. Ten clams a day. Et inna commizerry. Everybody have beer. Toast. Forget name of pitcher," he said, scratching his head. "Have'a go all cowboy pitchers now to see myself."

"What a dumbbell. He's inna pitcher and he don't even know the name of it."

"Drum-something. Scalped two whitemen. Almost scalped leading lady, but hero—he wore perfume all'a time—he come in last minute and cracks my skull open with a carbine. Gets the prize. Yawww, he can have it," he said, fumbling at the drawstring of the sack. "All she did was yap about the flies in the latrine and how hot it was and when were they gonna go home to Malibu—where-ever that is."

"I'm seeing things," said Capon, stepping away from the group and peering out in the distance. The others turned and stared hard in the same direction.

A snow-white Jaguar convertible, the top down, its long low body gleaming, the chrome bubbles of its headlamps glinting in the sun, bounced over the desert, leaving a wide, high wake of yellow dust behind it.

"What inna hell's zat?" said the Indian, bracing himself against the wall and trying to push himself up.

"Ain't you never seen no automobile?"

"Um, not without no highway under it."

"Must be lost."

"May be some of them movie people."

"If it's that friggin' leading lady," grumbled the Indian, falling down again, "I'm gonna hide."

"Coming like a bat outa hell. Hope its brakes are good."

"Looks like everybody's coming to our doorstep today," said Mex, rubbing his hands gleefully. "Think I oughta warm up the beans?"

"See first if it's friend or foe," said Hook.

At the wheel was a young woman wearing sunglasses, her dark hair flying in the wind. Beside her sat an older woman, her features blurred through the dusty windshield.

The car came straight on, without reducing speed until it got within a few yards of the men when the driver turned the wheel sharply, the car careening in a curve, the rear wheels spinning sand as she put on the brakes. The car rocked to an abrupt halt.

The young woman took off her sunglasses and looked at the men. They stood close in a group and looked back at her.

"Hey there, which way is the highway?" she called.

The men did not answer.

She turned to the woman beside her and shrugged her shoulders.

"Perhaps they don't speak English, dear," said the woman.

The girl's mouth went down at the corners as she surveyed the men again. Then she smoothed her hair, pulled on the emergency brake and stepped out of the car.

As she approached them she ruffled out the folds of her Mexican peasant blouse and the wrinkles in her slacks. On her feet were straw sandals.

"Don't touch them, Claudia!" called the woman from the car, in a hoarse whisper. "They might be diseased."

"Do you speak English?" said the girl as she came up to the men.

"Sort'a," said Hook.

"Gee, you sure are a far piece from the highway, mam," said Mex.

Hook and Capon laughed.

"What's so funny?" she asked with a perplexed expression. "The point is—how far is it and which way?"

"I'd sure like to know that, mam," said Hook.

"You mean you don't know?"

"Well, not yet, mam."

"That's a snappy looking automobile you got there," said Capon.

Mex, Capon and Hook wandered over to the car

and crowded around it, inspecting it closely. Morning Light sat with his head in his hands staring at the scene through slit eyes. William watched from the doorway, his hands in his pockets.

"Haven't you ever seen a car before?" said the older woman, as the men grouped around and looked into the interior. "Don't get too close."

She also wore dark glasses, blue rims festooned with plastic daisies; her thighs stuffed into aquamarine pedalpushers. On her head was a pink straw cap, tilted back, the name SUSIE stitched in letters on the inside of the peak.

"Don't touch anything," warned the girl, nervously.

Mex spelled out MIX with his finger in the dust on the fender.

"How come you're way out here?" said Capon, turning to the girl.

"If you really must know, I came out to sketch desert scenes—and Mother wanted to see the desert . . ."

"Oh, Claudia, you'll be the death of me with your insane notions!—Young man, you're breathing in my face. When was the last time you brushed your teeth?—Driving clean off the highway. When I'd only wanted to see the desert, *safely*, from 66. And now we don't know where we are!" she announced to the men. "Haven't seen a square inch of asphalt for miles."

"Hush, mama. This is the Twentieth Century, remember? Women are no longer the frail, helpless nonentities they used to be," she said, turning to the men. "Now, tell us, which way to the highway, if you please?"

"Which highway do you mean, mam?"

"Any one close by. At this point we aren't particular."

"Well, I'm the Nineteenth, dear," interrupted her mother, petulantly, her lips twitching. "And I beg you to remember that. You seem to have no consideration.—And you forget how hard I try to keep up with you."

"All right, mama, that's enough I say!" said Claudia, stamping her foot. "This heat's irritating enough without you feeling sorry for yourself. You wanted to see the desert and you're seeing it."

"Not a clean rest station for miles . . ." groaned her mother, fluttering a handkerchief at her throat.

"Well, if you insist upon being in one of your moods," said Claudia. She beckoned to the men. "If you'll just follow me we'll settle this business out of her hearing—as she seems to want to be by herself."

She reached into a leather pocket inside the car door and withdrew a sketch pad and a box of charcoal sticks.

"You always leave me out of everything," said her mother.

The men followed the girl to the hut, casting glances back at the car as they went.

"I might as well sketch the crew of you while I'm here. Except that lout," she said, pointing at the Indian. "You there, get out of the way. I want the rest of you to group yourselves before this enchanting hacienda. Something quaint and picturesque—primitive—about it all," she said, then leafed through the pages of her sketch pad as the men stood around staring dumbly at her.

"Well?" she said, glancing up. "Are you going to stand there like logs? Group yourselves—nothing stiff, a natural pose—to catch the desert-like flavor of you. The day of the daguerreotype still-life is over," she announced. She selected a stick of charcoal from the box and tested it on a corner of the paper.

Mex looked at the others and shrugged his shoulders.

"Hey, lady!" called the Indian, still slumped against the wall. "Where the hell's Malibu?"

"Why aren't you on the reservation, where you belong?"

"I gotta in with the warden. Any time I want a pass I sing 'God Bless America' five times unner his window—and I get out." He winked at her. "You wanta beer?"

"Ugh. And drunk as a fool. Isn't there a law against giving liquor to Indians?" she said, turning to the men.

"We haven't been in town for years, mam," said Hook. "We wouldn't know."

"I'd report it to the authorities, Claudia!" shouted her mother. "Hail the first state trooper we see on the highway. When we *get* to the highway. Hurry those men up with the information, dear."

"Hey there—you—black suit, you look like a cultivated man."

"Not me."

"Don't be modest," said Claudia, smiling. "I see you're not of the same cut as these hombres." She jerked her thumb at the others. "Own up."

"I've given up all that."

"What do you mean?"

"What I say."

"You mean you've thrown away your culture?"

"Such as it was. That, and other things."

"How queer. The rest of us spend so much money and time getting it and you just up and throw it away. Why?"

"I'd rather not say."

"Why not?" she persisted, advancing upon him, hands clasped loosely about her hips.

"It's so hot to argue. And you would only want to argue."

"You probably hadn't much to begin with, so it wasn't hard for you."

He was silent.

"Aren't you European?"

"No."

"You look European."

She studied his face. "Clean-cut features. Nose a bit too pointed for my taste. And the way that one ear sticks out—spoils the proportion. French, I'd say. Passable eyes, but a bit weak. Hazel?" She leaned into his face. "Yes. *Votre figure* would make a nice portrait. But doing portraits is old hat." She started to walk away and then turned to him again.

"Are you a man of the cloth?"

"Which cloth?"

"The table cloth?" chuckled Mex.

"The loincloth," muttered Hook.

"Out of my dark there sometimes shoots a ray of lucidity." He put his hand to his mouth. "No—that isn't what I want to say."

"What kind of talk is that? Who are you quoting? You look like a castoff parson from Chautauqua," she laughed.

"There's serene music there," said William. "And the old ladies, who won't die, sit on gingerbread porches reading slender volumes of Browning. I'm a stray dog, flirting with everyone—for a bone, a kiss. Right now I'm occupied in translating the Bible into good business English. I must rinse out my rhetoric, hold it up in the sun to dry." He bowed and turned away, biting his lower lip.

"You smell like a dog, that's for certain," sniffed Claudia, crinkling her nose. She brushed her long hair back over her shoulder. "Another of these effeminate Hamlets, always out of joint with the times. Think of nothing but their own selfish broodings. I'll inform you, since you seem so out of it, that this is the Twentieth Century. We care about our fellowman—whether he has enough to eat, whether he has proper living quarters and has decent working conditions. That through Art we shall lead him to an ennobling and better understanding of himself. You might think of that for a while instead of your sick, egocentric self. Open your eyes to the squalor these men live in. It would do you some good. We're no longer selfish or narrowminded. —We no longer forget or despise our fellowman— black, red, yellow or whatever he be."

"Would you sleep with a black man?" said William, his back still turned.

"Of course not!"

"Then how can you say you love him? Mustn't you then lie down with him, like St. Francis, if you truly believe what you say?"

"I'm speaking the new religion of awareness through the liberal ideal. An awareness of man's suffering and his pitiful ignorance. That beneath the skin we are all alike, struggling toward the ideal. Yes, I take back what I said. I would sleep with a Negro—a Negress, of course—to prove my point."

"A queer turn. A test-tube marriage with grinding

teeth. I smell Plato here. The idea loved more than the man, or your nigger wench, say—"

"Don't use that—!"

"How often we love man from afar when we can't stand the smell of him under our noses."

"All this doubletalk.—What are you, one of those unfrocked Jesuits, damned to roam your desert in search of your silly God? One of those hypocritical neo-Catholics. The new religion of the Twentieth—"

"Mum, mum, I have a seed in my tooth. Excuse me." William went to the hut and sat down, his head in his hands.

"He's been walking a long while in the heat," explained Mex. "He don't feel so good."

"Talks nonsense. Sounds like the sun fried his brainpan."

"Brains and eggs, that's a good breakfast," smiled Mex, rubbing his belly.

Claudia stared at him a minute and then, with a barely perceptible lift of her eyelids, turned and walked over to Hook.

"Claudia! Whatever's taking you so long?" Her mother, still seated in the car, held up a thermos bottle. "This is bone dry. Ask those men if they have any water."

"Give us some of your water," said Claudia to Hook. "You won't pose for me, you can't tell us the way to the highway, the only intelligent-looking one amongst you talks like an idiot, the least you can do is give us some water."

"Uh, uh."

"What? I ask for a little water and all you do is say 'eh-eh' and scratch your fleas."

"I have as much fleas as you have courtesy, mam."

"That's a pretty turn of speech. Now I'll give you one. I've as much fury as you have rudeness. Don't try me."

"Wanta try *me*?"

"I only want some water. My mother, poor dear, has asthma and her throat must be like sandpaper. Now just give me some safe, reliable H_2O."

"Not till you ask for it courteously, mam."

"I'm speaking to you in a civilized manner—"

"They didn't invite you here," bawled the Indian, lurching between them. "Whyn't you dance a different tune?"

"Your breath is putrid." She shoved him aside. "Look," she said to Hook, "just tell me where that water is and I'll get it myself. I'll show you I'm not helpless."

"It's there in the hut, but I wouldn't go in there alone."

"Why not?"

"Because I'm liable to follow you."

"What cheap nerve!" she cried, slapping his face.

"You get more discourteous by the minute, mam," said Hook, rubbing his cheek.

"Claudia!" called the mother. "What's the trouble? Hurry with the water!"

"These boors expect me to fall down on my knees to them to beg for a drop of their nasty water!" she called over her shoulder. "I won't do it!" she said, facing Hook.

"Drink your gasoline."

"I think I'd rather."

"Bet it's good-grade stuff. No rust on the pipes."

"It is, for your information. I buy nothing but the best."

"Claudia! Some water, will you?"

"Listen, at least for her sake. Can't you see she's an old woman?"

"Better not let her hear that," grinned Hook, nodding toward the car. "She seems kinda crabby on that point. You say 'please' for old ladies, too."

Hook turned on his heel and went behind the hut. Claudia, puzzled, watched him go, then ran her fingers through her hair and rubbed her eyes. She stared around at the other men who stared back at her silently. The Indian was dozing.

Hook came back a moment later, carrying a pint whiskey bottle in his hand.

"Is that water?"

"Smell it."

Claudia winced as he held the bottle out to her. She touched it with the tips of her fingers.

"Is it safe to drink? It's awfully tepid. What do you do, keep it out in the sun?"

"Mam, Lesson A," said Hook, spitting over his shoulder. "This is the desert. In the desert it's hot. Hot. You feel it? No. I'll go further. In the desert it's not only hot but there ain't no wells, ain't no clear running springs. Lesson B: the water'll cost you ten bucks."

"I won't pay it."

"No water then."

He tilted the bottle and emptied it; a damp mark remained in the sand where it splashed.

"Wait! Listen—I haven't got ten dollars."

"Haven't got? You'd better. Because listen: we got the water, we got the grub, we got the way to the highway. Therefore, we get you. Ten bucks. Cheap."

Claudia glared at him, then spun around and

walked quickly to the car. She yanked open the door and jumped in behind the wheel.

"Claudia! Whatever in the world! Did they say vile things to you?"

"Never mind, we're getting out of—. The key! Where's the ignition key?"

She turned to her mother and her mother shook her head, her mouth pursed, her eyes wide and frightened.

"I have it here, mam. In my watchpocket," said Hook, smiling, ambling up. He squatted and leaned his elbows on the sill of the car door. "I lifted it while I was inspecting your lovely dashboard."

"You beast! Two helpless women—!"

"That's right."

"O Claudia! Have we fallen amongst murderers?" cried her mother, grasping her daughter's arm in alarm.

"Not murderers, mam," said Hook, politely tipping his hat to her. "We are all lovers. All us gentlemen here are lovers," he swept his hand toward the group.

Mex came up, looking furtively at the women then at Hook. "I'd give her the water," he whispered, bending in Hook's ear. "She's kinda upset. And her mother's cheeks look like two red innertubes 'bout to blow out."

"Let 'em rip."

"Will you *please* give me the key."

"Oh good! She said it!" squealed Mex, clapping his hands. "Now you'll get everything."

"But so nasty," said Hook, making a face. "More sweet, huh?"

"Please," said Claudia, her fingers stretched loosely over the wheel.

"Ut, still an edge in it."

"Honestly, please, please, give me the keys."

He rose, bowed to the waist and, flourishing the key, placed it in her outstretched palm. She immediately inserted it in the ignition and started the motor.

"Aren't you even gonna thank me?" said Hook, hat in hand.

"The male conceit," snorted Claudia, stepping on the gas pedal and making the motor roar.

"Could, if I wanted to, take that key back," said Hook, wrapping his hand around the wheel. "Your arms are so pretty—so thin and fine. One twist— And—"

"Hurry, Claudia!" cried the mother, hugging the side of the door. "Let's get out of here!"

Claudia released the emergency brake and stamped on the gas, spinning Hook flat on his back, as the car tore off across the desert, moving in the direction it had come.

Hook got up and came back to the hut, jogging his limbs and grinning at the white cloud of dust, all that remained of the car and the two women.

"Makes you feel frisky," he said, slamming himself face down in the earth and rolling his body over and over.

"You let them get away like that?" said Capon, sticking his foot out, his heel catching Hook's hip and stopping him in the midst of one of his rolls. Hook sprang up, powdered with dust from head to toe, and throwing his arms around the other man, cried ecstatically, "They'll be back. Oh, they'll be back all right! Think that dame's got nose enough to smell her way to a highway? Think the afternoon's a time to nest her when there's the cool night coming? And she'll want a little heat. She'll want that—bad. Badder'n ever she wanted that water or the key to her car!" And he let the other man go and danced around with great hops, throwing his hat high in the air and catching it. "Man's gonna hafta fight mean'll crack that pearl!" he shouted, slamming his fist in the palm of his hand.

"Too much noise here," growled the Indian, thrusting himself up. He swayed to one side, falling to his knees. Then slowly got himself up again and staggered toward the arroyo. At the edge he collapsed and, crawling on his hands and knees, got down the slope. Rolling over on his back he slid himself beneath the car, elbowing the dog over to make room for his body. The dog whimpered in his sleep and squirmed up beneath the motor. The Indian folded his hands on his chest, his long feet sticking out under the rear bumper. Gurgling noises came from his throat. Soon he began to snore heavily.

The sun sank behind the far mesa. Immediately the air grew cool. The harsh light went out. Dusk filled the desert, deep shadows spread between the drifts of sand. The sky to the east was darkening and already a few stars showed. Mex lugged the cookpot out of the ashes and set it near the hut. The men sat down in a ring around, each taking turns putting in his hand, eating the beans cold. When the pot was empty, Mex brought wood from behind the hut and rebuilt the fire. The men watched as a train, the long length of it seen from engine to caboose, moved slowly across the plain, miles to the north.

The fire blazing, the men drew themselves up to it. Mex pulled out a packet of Jezebel cigarets, opened the lid, scooped out a handful and, thumbing them fanwise in his hand, offered them to the men, the gold tips spread outward.

"Them fairy fags," sneered Hook, turning his face and waving them away.

"You can have them perfume-sticks.—Me, I'll have a squint at Miss J. herself," said Capon, snatching the box out of Mex's hand. Holding it up in the fading light he stared, grinning, at the reclining figure of a buxom woman stamped in gold on the purple lid. Hook leaned over Capon's shoulder, staring at the print of the woman, then traced his finger slowly over the curve of her hip.

William took one of the cigarets, looked at it curiously, then put it between his lips as Mex lit a twig from the fire and, reaching over, lit first William's and then his own. The two men sat puffing quietly, the smoke filling the air with the scent of lavender.

"Makes both of you reek like two-bit whores," said Capon, sliding away from them and rubbing his nose briskly.

"More like some nickel cake of terlet soap," said Hook, tossing the packet back to Mex. "If the two of them was only real whores—now, I wouldn't mind."

"Whyn'a hell don't you smoke an American butt? Least that's a smell a man don't stick his nose up at."

"When the sun goes down," Mex leaned over and said to William, "and everything gets quiet, I like to put on my hat and smoke me a Jezzie. And I like to hear a good story. Hook and Capon here, they tell fine stories, but they're a little on the coarse side.—Now don't rile up you two."

"That's his tale, I'm sitting on mine," said Capon.

"Enough to raise the hackles on your back some-times," he whispered, putting his hand to the side of his mouth. "But a man once in a while likes to hear a different kind of a story. And I was wondering if—" He touched William's knee. "Do you know what I mean?"

"I don't know what story you'd want to hear," said William, glancing at him, then at the cigaret forked between his fingers.

"Aw, gwan, Rev," said Capon. "You can't be no worse'n me and Hook here—or that oily-mouthed spic there—for all he's trying to make hisself out to be a angel."

"I don't know," said William, looking around, embarrassed.

"Hell," said Hook, jumping up. "I'll get you some mescal and maybe that'll warm up your pipes." He went to the door of the hut and, pulling the blanket back, stepped inside. He came out a minute later carrying a tan jug over one shoulder. He squatted down again with the men, and holding the jug steady between the heels of his boots, leaned down and bit the cork out with his teeth.

"Here," he said, spitting the cork to one side and holding the jug out to William, "have a swallow, Rev."

William took the jug, stuck his nose in the opening, then lifting it in both hands, tilted the neck to his mouth, his adam's appple bobbing as he drank. Suddenly he thrust the jug from his lips, and clapping his hand over his mouth, began coughing and sneezing.

"You'll get the hang of it, bye and bye," said Capon, grinning at the others as he took the jug from William. He looped his thumb in the handle and, swinging the jug onto his forearm, tipped his head back and drank long and deep. Then he passed the jug to the others, while he snorted and brushed the palm of his hand back and forth under his nose.

"Burned my throat," said William, his eyes red and running. He blew his nose hard on his handkerchief.

"Good for the night chill," said Hook, swinging the jug to Mex.

Mex drank and then set the mescal in the middle of the circle, saying, "Now you got your vents cleaned out, Rev, you can go on with that story. Anytime you feel yourself running out of words, you're welcome to reach for the jug."

William crunched his cigaret in the sand. Folding his legs under him, he leaned his elbows on his knees and stared down at the ground for a moment. He lifted his head and said, "There was this young man, you see. And he roamed the streets of the city—unbathed for a week, and drunk as long, stubble on his face and nicks and slashes from unremembered falls. His wallet gone, in some alley. In crowds he kept his hands in his pockets. At night, wandering in some deserted side street, he'd come upon a stranger, some derelict, drunk like himself. He'd lean close to the stranger and say, 'You see, I have nothing. I've given it all up. All that.' And he would stumble away, as though in a hurry to get somewhere, but he had nowhere to go. Finally, exhausted and hungry, his bowels nothing but water, there wasn't anything to do now except to climb the five flights up to her door. He got up there somehow, the eyes of Puerto Rican children watching him curiously through the railings. At the top he almost pitched backward down the stairs but managed to swing himself around to slump against the wall. He waited til he got his breath and his heart stopped hammering and then rang the bell. The door opened and she stood there, dressed in a bathrobe, her hair tied behind. She looked at him, her hand moving up to her mouth. 'I—like—like—how are you, Mary?' he said. She helped him inside and sat him down in a chair. His head swung and his eyes tried to focus on her, his cracked lips moving, fluttering. 'I—I—like—I had meant to come—I—like—like how are you, Mary?' Broken, the words, and his head fell to his breast as she stood watching him, not speaking. He began to cry, dry wrenchings of his shoulders, his hands lying uncoiled on the arms of the chair, not even lifted to shield his face. Silently she stooped, unknotted his tie, unbuttoned his shirt. He began to protest: 'No—Mary—I, no—like—I—I—.' She went into the bathroom, turned on the hot tap in the tub and came back. Kneeling beside him, she removed his shoes and socks, unbuckled his trousers and slid them down. Then she leaned him forward in the chair and pulled off his coat, his shirt, slipped off his underwear. He sat naked in the chair. She folded his clothes neatly in a pile on the table. And all the while he was crying, softly pressing one dirty foot behind the other. She took his arm and helped him from the chair—and he followed her, stumbling, his face pressed in one shoulder, to the bathroom. The tub was full and she turned off the tap, helped him over the side, holding him firmly around the waist as he slid down into the water. He looked at her, trying again to speak, his hands swaying in the water. She placed her hand over his mouth, soaped the cloth and started with the face, gently over the crusts of blood, then his ears, his neck, his arms, the rest of his body, the water turning gray to darker gray. She refilled the tub and rinsed his body with a sponge, helped him from the tub and dried him with a soft towel. She rubbed oil in his cuts. Taking a robe from behind the door, she placed it over his shoulders and led him out and to a bed, the fresh sheets turned down. He lay down and she pulled the covers over him. He watched her move above him, her palms smoothing the sheet. 'Mary—I—Mary—' His hand moved out from beneath the coverlet, reached to touch her. She leaned over, kissed his lips, his eyes, turned out the light and left, closing the door quietly behind her."

He stopped speaking and looked around at the faces staring at him, quiet, waiting. He cleared his throat. The light had gone out of the sky.

"Well—go on," urged Mex.

"That's all," he said, shrugging his shoulders. "That's all I have to tell."

"Well, that was real fine," said Mex, blowing his nose between his fingers."

"Something stuck in his craw, eh?" said Hook.

"Wash it down with another drink," said Capon, giving the jug to William.

William drank. The jug again made the round of the circle.

"That was a woman," said Hook.

"Women," said Capon, "women, women," his arms out before him, his fingers hooked as though to embrace something in the air. "I like to touch the hollows of their throats."

"Look."

A hush fell over the men. The red moon rose over the desert.

"The itch of the moon."

"Pretty thing though."

"A torment."

"Rev, you talk like a disappointed man."

"Thump! down the chute."

"Life's a fine thing," said Mex, touching his arm.

"My tongue forgets itself."

"Let's don't make this a wake," said Hook grabbing the jug. They drank again as the moon shed fine red light over the sands.

William's eyes went bright and slight tremors ran over his body. He jumped up and began walking up and down before the men in short quick steps, agitated, rubbing his knuckles in the palm of his other hand.

"You feeling horny, mister?" said Hook, leaning for the mescal.

"The Indian, where is he?" cried William, swinging sharply upon the men. "He'll teach us the old dances of the earth. The ancient songs."

"Take it easy, Billy boy."

"Morning Light?" guffawed Mex. "He's a jazzer. Oughta see him bounding around enough to break a leg outside the dancehall of a Saturday night. Quart of whiskey in him and you can't hold him down."

"Not that," blurted William. The pulse of his heart beat visibly in the tight muscles of his throat. He began pacing again, back and forth, crunching his heels heavily in the sand.

"Mescal's took," chuckled Hook. He took another swig from the jug.

William stepped over the shoulders of Capon and

Hook and walked off in the direction of the arroyo. The others looked at each other, questioningly, then back at William who was trotting down into the arroyo, his footsteps sending up puffs of dust.

The men got up and followed him. Mex brought the jug.

When they got down in the bottom of the dry riverbed, they saw William squatting behind the rear of the car, his hands wrapped around the ankles of the Indian, tugging to pull him out from beneath.

"Come out! Dance!" he cried, pulling hard on the Indian's legs. Sweat ran down his face.

"You men!" he shouted, dropping one leg. "Give me a hand. Drag him out! Make him dance."

The men came over and grouped around him. Hook stooped over and, cupping his hands to his mouth, sang softly, "Arise, O Morning Light!"

The men howled.

The loose foot slid slowly beneath the car and disappeared, then suddenly it shot out, the force of the kick catching William square in the stomach. The other foot flew from his hand and he pitched backward in the sand, groaning and clutching his fingers tight to his belly.

"Leave a man alone," came a muffled voice from beneath the car's body. The legs drew themselves under.

The others went over and picked William up.

"That'll teach you, gringo," laughed Hook, slapping the dust off William's buttocks.

"Don't never fool with a drunk Indian," said Mex, trying to unbutton William's shirt. "Did he bust your gut?"

"No!" cried William, thrashing out at them with his arms, his face contorted as though he were about to cry. He broke away and stood staring down at the motionless feet jutting out. "That's not the white man's music," he gasped.

"That's right," said Capon, walking over and putting his hand about William's neck. "Old proverb 'bout the dead Indian's still true. But we can't kill 'em, legal, anymore. And so you let 'em drink themselves to sleep and you let them be. 'Cause Morning Light, he's as good as dead that way, or any Indian. Right now, that's the only good Indian."

"I'll invent the dance," said William. He tossed off Capon's arm and walked away. A few yards from the car he dropped down on his hands and knees and began searching in the dust.

The men laughed, then each took turns tipping the jug to his throat. After they drank they walked over and watched William picking around on the ground.

"What you scratching like a hen for?" laughed Capon.

"Chick, chick, chick," sang Mex, walking around William and swinging his arm as though he were scattering feed.

Hook let out an earsplitting cockcrow.

William got up, holding a twig of dead brush in his hand. "Sit down, sit down," he said, motioning to the ground.

"Whatcha gonna do, preach us a sermon, Rev?"

The men sat down on the ground, snorting with laughter and elbowing each other in the ribs.

"Hope he don't pass the hat," yelped Capon.

"We're each gentlemen of the flesh," said William, flourishing the twig.

"Amen," crowed Hook.

"A mouthful, brother, a mouthful."

"This root is my magic stick," said William, holding it up between thumb and forefinger. "I'll conjure it to bud.—From the shriveled pores of it, watch the green shoots pop. Believe, believe, my fingers are suns."

"Looks like a piece a' poor dead drift to me," chuckled Mex, winking at the others.

"Damned stick!" cried William. He flung the twig at the sky and held his hands up before his face. "My fingers are wands."

"Conjure us up a woman, Rev."

"Throw him your Jezzies, Mex. Let him bring that babe to life."

"Rev, you ain't talking sense like a white man. You talking jug-sense."

"Tic of the tongue," said William. He tugged at the cloth of his trousers. "This is heavy." He dropped to the sand, quickly unlaced his shoes and kicked them off, then tore off his socks. "Off with our clothes, gentlemen. We'll make the dance," he said, removing his coat.

"I'm for that," said Hook, unzipping his levis.

"We can take our weekly flea-bath," laughed Mex.

Laughing and jostling each other, the men threw off their clothes and scattered them about the banks of the arroyo.

"Let 'em air out!" shouted Capon, as he heaved his boots in the air. They landed some yards away, plomping in the dust. "Phew! What a smell."

William ripped off his shirt and threw it aside, then dropped his trousers and stepped out of them.

He stood naked facing the other naked men. They were horseplaying, scooping up handfuls of dust and rubbing it in each other's armpits. They pinned Mex to the ground and, while Capon held him, Hook smeared his face with dirt, then rolled him over and dusted his buttocks, rubbing it in. Mex pounded the ground with his fists, tears running from his eyes with laughter, his fat shoulders quaking. He broke away from the other two and dragging himself off, sat up and began pelting them with handfuls of sand. Hook and Capon advanced on him, throwing sand back at him, until they stood over him. Then each scooped both hands in the dirt and poured handful after handful on top of his head.

"We'll dance!" cried William. "We'll dance now."

"You mean like this?" hooted Hook, and he leaned forward from the waist, and, beating the flat of his hand against his mouth, began whooping, his feet trudging the earth as he stamped around and around in a circle. Capon and Mex filed behind him, naked except for their hats, bending their bodies down and then arching back, a hand beating at their lips, their bodies streaked with dirt, hair hanging in their faces. They raised the dust with their treading feet, the deep howlings in their throats breaking the night silence.

"No, no," said William, waving his hands anxiously. He ran up to them and tried to break up the dance, but they shoved him aside, laughing and yelping, and continued to move around in a swaying, drunken circle. William turned away.

Exhausted, the men fell to the ground, lying flat on their backs, panting with laughter, sweat covering their bodies.

"Just like at the trading post," gasped Capon.

"Hell, better," said Hook, lifting himself and wiping the sweat from his eyes. "We oughta put on a show of our own out there some time for them tourists."

He slapped Capon's thigh and broke into laughter.

The other two sat up, rubbing their forearms across their brows and breathing heavily.

"Whew!" said Mex, taking a deep breath. "Sure dried up my wind whistle."

He walked over to the jug, his heavy haunches jiggling.

"Walks like a fat whore," snickered Hook.

Mex brought back the jug, took a long drink and gave it to the others.

"That's the spirit!" shouted Capon. He snatched the jug, his lips sucking thirstily at the neck.

"Don't drain it," said Hook, tapping him on the shoulder. And as Capon continued to drink, Hook pulled the jug from his mouth and thrust it to his own.

"Sure fixes me good," grinned Capon, running his tongue around his lips. "Foo! Damn grit," he said, making a face and spitting the sand from his mouth.

"We'll need some of this for the ritual," said William, coming over and laying his hand on the jug.

"Why sure, Reverend, sure," said Hook, handing it to him. "You gonna baptize us?"

The men laughed. Then they grew quiet, breathing more easily, and watched as William held the jug close to his ear and shook it.

"Empty," he said, letting the jug swing loose at his hip.

"Need water for a baptism, do you?" said Hook, hopping up. "I'll make water." He urinated, the splattering stream quickly sucked into the dust.

"Blood's thick and will hold," said William. He

swung the jug over his head and the others ducked
as he brought it down upon a rock, shattering it.
Picking up a jagged shard of the splintered jug, he
sat down and began slicing crosses in the soles of
his feet.

The men watched him, tensed, their eyes wide.

"Thirsty earth," he said, the palm of his hand
caressing the dust. "My blood, ghost-appeaser."
He squeezed blood from his feet onto his fingertips
and sprinkled the dust. "Will they speak to me
now?" He stared down at the drops of blood, the
dust coating and making little balls of it. He
clapped his hands to his head. "My ears smoke
awaiting the word. My eyes, for the apparition."

The men sat motionless, their mouths slightly
parted, watching his every move.

"She comes," crooned William, rocking back and
forth. "Is it you?" he asked suddenly, staring dis-
believing at the air. "Queen's robes, gray and root-
clotted from the grave. My sight blurs." He gave
his head a quick shake. "Are those seedpearls down
the folds?" His hand reached out, the fingers uncoiling slowly, began to brush at the air. "Why
don't you speak?" he cried angrily, peering as
though at someone before him. "Dumb mouth a
hole of grief. Why do you hold your arms so? To
chase crows? How they fill the air, wings beat,
black and silken." He flailed his arms about and
pressed his chin to his chest, gritting his teeth. He
looked up, his hands fluttering over his head, his
eyes fearful, as he peered around at the sky.
"Gone?" He gradually let his arms fall. His eyes
focused again before him. "Listen," he said in a
harsh voice, crooking his finger, "Close, close—I'm
falling asleep, Mother—It's no good." He slumped

down in the sand, his lids closing. "The great bird hovers," he murmured. "Alights on my belly, its claws dig into my flesh, its beak sinks straight into my middle!" he shrieked, kicking his legs, his mouth straining, the muscles in his hands taut as they cupped themselves over his stomach. "It's pulling the guts from me, it's lifting me from the bed, the wings shudder over me, drawing me up." He sat erect. His eyes snapped open. "No blood?" he said, huskily, running his fingertips over the skin. He dropped his gaze. "Your arms must be tired," he breathed softly. "A little blood to refresh you." Clutching a foot in his hand, he ran a finger up the sole and whipped blood off at the air. "Let them fall. I'm so tired, Mother," he sighed. His shoulders sagged, his hands twitched on his thighs. "I'm in the bed of the river. Lift me, lift me up. Bring me into the light. Mother, I'm so old, so old and tired. Give me the light. Don't touch me!" He reared back, holding his hands up before him to fend off some invisible thing. "No more of your dry lips. Disintegrate to dust. Don't—yet!" He gesticulated with his hands, desperately motioning something back. "Mother—listen—I'm not anything. Not any of that. I want to be quiet. I'm William-eyes and William-ears. I'm William-mouth and William-heart. Poor dumb cock!" he cried, seizing his groin. "Barbs forged in hell's red belly. There, through smoke, the glamorous jew squints spanishly at me. Lights in his eyes, he says. Brambles, say I."

He pressed his knuckles deep into sockets.

"Ah ah ah," he whispered. "Ah ah ah."

"Take it easy," croaked a voice from the men.

"To sleep?" he asked, staring out, wild-eyed. "Enough of that." His fingers dumbly stroked the sand. "Only now I see I slept all my years beneath layers of silt." He scooped up some of the blood-moist dust and kneaded it between his fingers. "My soul is blond. Ribs nesting fire. How late it gets. Smash time. Beware those razors in their eyes. They slice you. Hard-won innocence of manhood," he murmured, scattering the dust from his hand. "To bust through—a fist to punch with!" He sprang up and stepped toward the men, his feet tracking prints of themselves, damp in the sand. "I want that," he whispered fiercely, leaning over them. "The sick exhaust me. The body," he said, with awe, running his hands down himself and staring around at the dark. "A man could walk forever out there, his body aching. Christ yap," he said, his fist banging his thighs. "Redskin!" he shouted to-ward the car. "Dance! Og! He's drunk, the dance sprung from his arches." He walked with measured steps up and down before the men, his heels kicking the dust lightly. "Nevermind nevermind nevermind. Cool gringo—jazz-song—jazz-dance—to it, to it."

He looked around at their faces as though he did not see them, then furtively back over either shoulder, his body trembling. "I see I'm on dangerous ground. Fears press in to snap the spine. No turning back. Broken—cold acid leaks in the bones. A corner of cloth to cover—there and there. Wake me before dawn."

Entranced, he rubbed his hands across his chest, staining the skin with blood. He moved toward the men.

"Princes, you are all princes. Above all, don't be afraid. Don't desecrate the wonder. No more nightmares. Walk dreamful in the day. Splendid peoples. Move us as tides, eyes open."

His hand went to his throat and his lids fluttered. "I see I've been dreaming," he said, and fainted, falling face down in the sand.

Mex ran to him and turned him over. He lifted him by the shoulders and propped his head on his knee.

"Mescal finally hit him over the head," said Capon. He got up and walked over. Hook followed him. They stared down at the unconscious man.

From the edge of the arroyo the beams of a car's headlights cut through the darkness, illuminating the naked bodies in a white glare. The men stared up, blinded, into the lights. The car banked abruptly, the wheels spinning in the earth, sending down a great spray of sand over the men below. It jerked forward, swerving over the sand, then, as the wheels dug in, it shot in a straight line across the desert. Above the roar of the motor on the still night came the sharp screams of women.

"Them?" coughed Capon, beating the dust out of his eyes.

"You shoulda told them, Hook," said Mex, sneezing, his eyes watering.

"They shoulda knowed."

"No water."

"It's cool now."

The dust settled.

"Come on, Cape! You can have the old lady!" shouted Hook, running for the touring car.

"We'll see about that," said Capon, snatching up his hat and planting it on his head. "You watch out for the invalid," he called over his shoulder. "We'll give you a smell when we get back."

Hook stooped down and cranked the motor, which started with an abrupt explosion, rocking the body on its springs. The dog bolted out from beneath and stood a few yards off, its hair bristled, thin high howls coming out of its throat. The motor hummed down to a steady, quiet knocking, the fenders and headlamps rattling with the vibration. Hook tossed his boots in the back and jumped behind the wheel. Capon sprang up beside him. The car strained up the slope of the arroyo, exposing the prone body of the Indian lying between the tire tracks left in the dust, his hands thrashing in his sleep. Once over the edge, it coughed along in the direction the other had gone, the tattered remains of the canvas top fluttering behind. Capon, naked, except for his hat, clutched the top of the windshield with both hands and leaned far out over the hood, straining to see through the thick dust the other car had made.

"The turtle and the rabbit," sighed Mex, letting his arms fall from his hips. He watched the car, the sound of the motor growing faint as it moved away, then he turned as it disappeared in the dust. He reached down and lifted William in his arms and carried him up out of the arroyo and back to the fire which was now a heap of smoldering coals. He lay William down close to it, then kicked up the coals with his heels and threw on more wood. He went into the hut and came back with a blanket, spread it on the sand and rolled William into it, then wrapped the blanket about him. The dog trotted up to the fire and lay down, shivering, and curled himself near the flames. Mex went behind the hut and brought back a clay bowlful of water. He paused and peered out to where the car had gone, then set the water down at the foot of the blanket and, kneeling, uncovered William's feet.

Unknotting the large bandana from around his neck, he dipped it in the water, wrung it out, and began carefully wiping at the crusts of blood and dirt on the soles of the feet. William cried out in his sleep and tried to draw his legs up into the blanket, but Mex held them firmly by the ankles and kept dabbing gently until he had scraped the crud away. Then he rinsed out the rag and wiped the soles of the feet clean. He leaned back on his heels and surveyed the feet, clucking his tongue and shaking his head. He looked around, then seeing the cactus, went over and stood running his fingers down the sleeve of the shirt hanging there.

"Hook'll have my ass," he said and whisked the shirt down. Bringing it back to the fire, he began tearing it into long strips. These he bound around William's feet. The dog came over and began lapping the dirty water. Mex put his hand over the dog's face and shoved him away.

"Git disaterry," he said and, lifting the bowl, heaved the water away into the darkness. He tucked William's feet into the blanket and then sat down before the fire, close to the dog, and began stroking the animal's throat.

The moon, now high in the sky, poured white light over the desert.

Soon he heard a motor and, looking, saw the touring car returning, the far, dim headlamps throwing a faint light before it. Capon stood on the runningboard, kicking one leg out and waving his hat. Suddenly the car swerved to the left and started going around and around in wide circles, Hook turning the wheel sharp first one way and then the other, making the car zigzag and kick up mounds of dust.

"Yip! Yip!" came the voice of Hook, clear and far away over the quiet night.

"Yip!"

"Spur 'er, Hook—gash blood from 'er!" came Capon's voice, deep and distant.

Hook swung the car through a series of crude figure eights, the car careening over the sand, the dust rising white and powdery as smoke in the moonlight.

"Yip!" came, like shrieks. "Yip! Yip!"

Hook cut the wheel hard and the car tipped to one side on two wheels, balanced there an instant, then thudded down with a loud groan on its springs. He put it in reverse and it shot backward. Then, the gears grinding, he steered the car toward the hut, the engine sputtering and missing.

Mex stepped from the fire to meet them but the car kept on coming and he jumped out of its path as it bore down on him.

"Hey! Where you going?" he shouted as it roared past him. Capon leaped, startled, from the running-board and fell to his knees on the ground, as Hook, hunched over the wheel, his teeth clenched, his eyes narrowed, headed straight for the hut. The car rammed the wall and shuddered to a halt. There was a trickle of spilling liquid somewhere beneath the car, then silence.

Mex came running over, and Capon, pulling himself up, followed, rubbing his shins.

Hook squeezed himself out from behind the wheel and stepped nimbly to the ground, a bruise swelling to a lump on his forehead, his lower lip split and bleeding.

"Old whore!" he shouted, booting a mangled fender. "Won't do no more'n thirty-five per hour."

"You hurt bad?" said Mex, peering at him.

"The-oh-whore!" shouted Hook, spitting on the motor standing upright out of the hood. "That's your name!" He smashed the crumpled hood down with his fists. "We'll straighten you out in the morning," he said, turning on his heel. "I'm gonna crap out."

He snatched his boots from the rear seat and stalked over to the doorway, whipped the blanket aside and went in. Mex and Capon stood listening to him stamp around, muttering curses, then the heavy thump of the boots heaved against the wall, the last jingle of the spurs ringing tinnily. Then all was quiet.

"Guess it's okay to go in," said Capon. He walked around the wreck, inspecting it. "To treat her like that just 'cause she ain't got no more pep. And, hell, it ain't like he rolled her off the floor yesterday.—To be so mad 'cause she busts a gasket doing thirty.—And who wouldn't, taken the beating she's took all her life."

"Hook'll like fixing her up," said Mex.

"I'm gonna turn in," said Capon. "Prob'ly woulda got the ole lady anyhow," he mumbled, disappearing into the hut.

When Mex returned to the fire, he saw the Indian squatting over the flames, his hands thrust to the warmth.

"Whata commotion out here," he yawned, as Mex came up. He shook his head, his eyes puffy with sleep. "Coo-coo fades," he muttered. "I'm gone back to town."

"How you feel, Morning?" said Mex, tossing a stick on the fire.

"Head like thirteen heads," he said, scratching his scalp. "All concrete."

William sat bolt upright, the blanket falling away

from his shoulders. "Still night?" he said, staring up at the sky.

"Them the best stockings he got?" said the Indian.

"He stepped on a mesquite bush," grinned Mex.

William looked around him with strained eyes. He saw the Indian and then Mex, and drew the blanket up about him.

"Shut your eyes before you bleed to death," said the Indian.

"I've got to go," William said. He struggled to get up. "I've got to get out of here." He got to his feet and immediately fell down, wincing and clutching his ankles.

"I scraped off the mess," said Mex. "You oughta rest up here a while."

"Where're my clothes?" he asked.

"Clothes are still down there," said Mex.

"You gone to town? I'm gone to town," said the Indian. "You come with me." He shuffled off behind the hut.

"You oughta stay here," said Mex. "Let your feet heal."

"I've got to push on."

Mex shrugged his shoulders. "It's your skin." He went down into the arroyo and picked up William's clothes and his own and came back just as the Indian was leading his horse out from behind the hut.

William put on his shirt. Then Mex helped him slide into his trousers as he lay on the blanket.

"Better carry your shoes and socks. Won't do to put them on yet."

Mex started putting on his own clothes.

"What you guys nekkid for?" said the Indian, adjusting the saddle strap on the horse. "Think night's hot as day?"

"Little party," said Mex, stepping into his dunga-rees.

"Party and no women," said the Indian, slapping the horse's belly. "I don't know what to think of that."

Mex laughed.

The Indian climbed onto the horse. "You get on behind me," he said to William.

William walked on his heels to the horse. "Put these here," said the Indian, reaching down and taking his shoes and socks from him. He lifted the flap of the saddlebag and dropped them inside. Mex boosted William and William swung onto the back of the horse. He placed his arms around the Indian's waist.

"Ready?"

"All set," said Mex. "Good luck there, Reverend," he said, touching the calf of William's leg.

William's head had fallen against the Indian's neck and he was asleep.

"I'll talk to myself," said the Indian. "Gee-up," he clucked, tugging at the reins. The horse started off at a slow walk.

"And you, Morning, you come again," said Mex, walking alongside.

The Indian grunted and Mex stood still, hands on hips, and watched as they went off, William's head bobbing on the other's shoulder. He watched until they had gotten quite a distance away and then turned and walked back to the fire. He stood a moment gazing around at the horizon. To the east was a faint flush of light. He threw more wood on the fire. He looked around once more, then dropped down on the blanket and, tipping his hat over his eyes, rolled himself up for sleep.

The Truck

Wally lifted the canvas flap and looked out the backend of the truck across the vacant lot toward 26th Street. It was getting dark. The streetlights hadn't been turned on yet and he squinted his eyes, leaning far out over the tailgate to get a better look.

"Man, ain't he coming yet?" said Muskrat. Muskrat was hunched up in a corner of the truck, his baseball cap pushed back on his head. On two board seats held up by cinderblocks sat Gyp the Greek and Little Joe, and Hector and Lipper. They were playing poker for pennies.

"He ain't gonna come back," said The Greek, raking in a pot with one big hairy paw. "He'll take the money and skidaddle."

"That's how much you know," said Wally. "I see him coming now."

"You better look again," said Little Joe. "Hard to tell a smoke in this light."

"It's Rosemary all right," said Wally, lifting the flap again and looking out.

A tall, lean Negro was walking slowly across the lot toward the truck, a bulging brown paper bag held in one arm.

"Manochrist! Open that canvas wide," Muskrat said. "It stinks like sneaker crud in here."

"Ain't nobody wearing sneakers in here," said Little Joe, flipping a fresh hand around the board,

172

supported on the knees of the players. "Excepting you."

"Hmmm, now ain't that a fact. Well, well."

"Shut up and do something useful," said The Greek. "Light us the lantern. I can't see the cards in front of my face."

"As if it being lighty made any difference," Lipper giggled.

The Greek reached over and gave Lipper a stiff rabbit punch on the arm.

"Shut up," he said. "You're jealous 'cause I don't go behind the billboards with you anymore."

"Ah, come off it," said Lipper, rubbing his sore arm. "You know I don't go behind the billboards anymore."

"Yeah, yeah," grunted The Greek. "You're one of the gang now. We know all about it."

"Come on, you guys," snapped Wally. "Stop the messing around. You wanta knock the truck off the blocks or something?"

"He started it."

"The hell I did!" The Greek said, rising from his seat and causing the truck to lurch to one side.

"Don't jiggle around, you guys, I said. You wanta knock the truck over?" Wally leaned down and pushed The Greek into his seat.

"Okay, okay. Just tell him to be careful."

"Man, let there be light!" shouted Muskrat. He swung a lantern up on a hook in the slatted ceiling of the truck. The flame spit weakly a few times, then leaped and held, burning with a steady, yellow glare.

"Isschibibblioo—eck! eck!" came from the outer side of the canvas flap.

"It's Rosemary," said Hector.

"That fruity shine's nuts. Don't pay attention to him," The Greek said.

"He gets the wine, don't he?" said Wally. "That's more'n you do."

"Yeah, but has he got it?"

A thin black face, sweaty and glistening in the lamplight, poked through the canvas flap.

"Tootie-patootie-skitzafrooti! I heard what you said, Gyp lover."

"Get outa here, you black pussy."

"Raggle-taggle ookliai—Dreadful—Dreadful."

"Man, drop that African nigger talk," said Musk-rat. "Whyn't you talk like an American nigger? You get the wine?"

"Kiss and tell," said Rosemary, shyly.

"Drag him in here," said The Greek. "Let's de-pants him and see what it is."

"Isschibibblioo—eck! eck!" piped Rosemary, thrusting the bag into Wally's hands. "I'm virgin timber-imber."

"You're nuts, if you ask me," said The Greek.

"Who's asking?" snapped Rosemary. "Waa-waa. Can I come in?"

"It's too crowded," said The Greek.

"Yummie!"

"Get outa here. I don't want no black hands pawing me."

"Let Rosemary alone," said Wally, unscrewing the lid from a bottle.

"Yeah, you guys, Wally's gotta crush on Rose-mary," said Lipper.

"Just let him alone," said Wally. He tilted the bottle to his lips and swallowed.

"What else you expect since he don't go behind the billboards with you anymore?" said The Greek. "You're jealous, Lipper."

"Can that stuff, will you?"

"Man, what the hell kinda poison is this?" said Muskrat, choking and gagging as he pushed the bottle at The Greek.

"Port, honey. Port's all I could get with what you gave me. I tried hard, baby, I really did. I look into that man's big blue eyes and I say, 'Honey, you sure we can't fix up something between what I got here and what you got there—I mean, to make up the difference, honey,' I says. But he's so crazy dumb he don't dig me at all. So I had to settle for port."

"Man, you need a castiron stomach to pipe it. I'd like to puke."

"Can I come in?" said Rosemary.

"Jump up," said Wally. "You'll have to sit on the tailgate though."

"And hold open the flap," said Muskrat. "It stinks in here."

Wally took Rosemary's hand and helped him to climb up. Rosemary sat down very quietly on the edge of the tailgate, crossing his long, thin legs and taking from his pocket a mashed rose. He sniffed at it and looked from face to face.

"Rosi-osi-prettiosi," he said, and waved the rose in front of him. "Stinking air's bad for the lungs."

"If you don't like it, get out," said The Greek. "Whyn'ahell don't one of us hurry up and get to be twenty-one, so we don't have to put up with this smoked fairy?"

"Gyp don't like me," said Rosemary. "He's such a man I make him doubt him."

"Go on, Gyp, and play cards," said Wally. "Don't try starting anything." He took a long swallow from the bottle and passed it around again.

Rosemary dropped the rose into his shirtfront

and took a liqueur flask from his hip pocket. A smell like sweet apples filled the truck. Rosemary sipped a little now and then from the flask.

"Drink some of this rotgut, Rosemary," Wally said. "And throw away that holy water."

"Afrateesiackalo—no—no," said Rosemary, taking another little sip of liqueur.

"For Christssake, Rosemary," said Muskrat. "You sound like you just got off the boat. Where'd you pick up that African lingo?"

"It ain't African. It's that bebop junk he picks up at the Dance Spot," said The Greek, not looking up from his cards.

"Nigger, nigger, on the wall," said Rosemary. "An' I can go pee in a white john anytime I please."

"If you got the nickel," said Muskrat.

"I got the nickel-lickel-o," said Rosemary. He smacked his lips after another small sip.

"I know where you get them nickels," said The Greek, tossing another penny into the pot. "I seen you hanging around inside that subway head in Philly."

"Have *you* got a nickel?" said Rosemary.

"Never you mind," said The Greek. "I know where you get your nickels."

"Penny-enny-enny, Gyp lover."

"Black fairy bastard!"

"Sticks and stones, Gyp lover."

They killed the first bottle and Wally opened the second, swallowed some and passed it around. It was getting dark outside. A streetlamp burned on each of the two corners of the lot. A couple of moths flapped around the lantern. The Greek slapped at a mosquito, then shuffled the cards, halving the deck, the cards making a ripping noise between his thumbs. He cut the deck himself and started spinning the cards around the board.

"No more for me," said Little Joe. "Let's do something else."

"What the hell, after I get them dealt and all that. What's the matter? You guys sore 'cause I'm taking all your money?"

"I'm tired of cards."

"Me, too," said Hector.

"G'wan," said The Greek, gathering the cards together and inspecting each of the hands he had dealt. "You're both sore 'cause I took all your money."

"Can it," said Hector. He took a cigaret butt from behind his ear and lit it, then leaned back and eyed The Greek.

"Whatta you mean 'can it'?" The Greek said, twisting his mouth to one side and staring at Hector, tough-like.

"Just what I said."

"Lay off, Gyp," Wally said. "You're always trying to start trouble."

"*Me* start trouble?" said The Greek, raising his voice. "*They're* the soreheads!"

"Man, can't we have peace in this frigging truck for one night?" said Muskrat. "Sometimes I wisht I *was* back in Jamesburg the way you guys yackety-yackety-yack like a bunch of crabbing women. Take a swig of the bottle, Gyp, and button up."

"Everybody's always yapping at me!" shouted The Greek. "Nobody tells me what to do!"

He lifted an empty wine bottle over his head, striking the lantern and shattering it. Everybody ducked, each throwing his hands over his head. The truck was in darkness. For a moment there was silence. You could hear The Greek breathing heavily and then the truck began to lurch from side to side as though The Greek was rocking himself back and forth, from wall to wall, in the darkness. The old truck springs creaked and ground noisily on the cinderblocks.

"Man, you'll turn us over you don't quit that," said Muskrat.

Rosemary giggled and slid off the tailgate to the ground.

"Let me outa here!" said Lipper, pushing his way to the canvas flap. "The Greek's rammy again."

Wally leaped to the ground and held the flap open. Lipper climbed out and the rest followed. They stood around the tailgate looking into the dark, still-rocking truck.

"You think he'll throw a fit?" said Muskrat.

"I don't give a damn," said Wally. "He's always lousing things up. Come on outa there, Gyp!"

There was no answer. The truck swayed violently now, then tipped to one side, balanced precariously for an instant on two wheel-less hubs. Each boy held his breath. The truck crashed down, righting itself. The creaking stopped, the truck resting quietly on the cinderblocks.

"Come the hell out of there, Gyp!" said Wally.

They heard The Greek stumbling around inside the truck. He fell heavily and lay still for a moment, cursing and muttering to himself. Then he started crawling to the rear of the truck where he flung half his body over the tailgate and vomited. The boys jumped back.

"Jesus Christ! On that teeny bit of wine," said Hector. "The strong man, yeah."

Wally and Muskrat took hold of The Greek under the armpits and hauled him down to the ground.

"Man, I don't feel like dragging this bulk up to 33rd Street."

"Nuts, let him lay there till he sobers up," said Little Joe. "Less us go sneak in on the second show up the 'Vic'."

"It ain't right to let him lay here like this," said Wally. "S'posing a cop comes along?"

"That's his toughluck," said Hector.

"What dear, true, everlasting friends," said Rosemary, mincing out of the shadows. "Hmph! I'll cart him home myself."

Rosemary leaned down and pulled The Greek up into a sitting position, then pulled out a handkerchief and wiped The Greek's sweaty face. The Greek moaned and his head fell back, his mouth flapping open. A trickle of saliva ran down his chin.

"Excuse me, baby," said Rosemary, and he began slapping The Greek hard on either cheek until The Greek's head rocked back and forth.

"Careful, man. You'll turn him over," snickered Muskrat.

"I'm okay, I'm okay," mumbled The Greek.

Rosemary wiped the spit from The Greek's chin and helped him to his feet.

"Lean, baby, lean," said Rosemary, throwing The Greek's arm around his neck to prop him.

The two started walking away across the lot, The Greek hanging onto Rosemary and Rosemary with one arm slung around The Greek's middle, holding him up.

"S'long," Wally called. But Rosemary didn't answer. He was talking all the time to The Greek and The Greek was grunting and saying, "I'm okay, I'm okay."

Lipper cupped his hands to his mouth and shouted, "Some Greek he-man, yeah! Put the baby to bed, Rosemary."

"Watch he don't burp on you!" shouted Little Joe, and turning to the others said, "Can you imagine? Just on that little stinking bit of wine?"

"That was mighty white of Rosemary," said Muskrat. "You guys oughta be ashamed of yourself." He flopped on the ground near the truck. "Christ, what a stink that guy left," he said, covering his nose with his hand. He crawled farther away and lay flat on his back, pulling his baseball cap over his face.

"Man, that wine sure knocks me for a dingdong."

"I didn't ever like The Greek," said Hector.

"Nor me," said Lipper. "He won't ever lay off to me about them billboards. Hell, I was only a little kid then. I don't see what he's gotta keep bringing it up like it's still happening or something."

"To hell with The Greek," said Little Joe. "Less us go sneak in on the second show up at the 'Vic'. We ain't done that in a helluva long time."

"What's on?" said Wally.

"Hell, I don't know. Whatsat matter? Less go."

"Oh, what the hell," said Wally. "The wine's out. You coming, Muskrat?"

"Man, I'm so bushed I feel like sleeping till doomsday. That old Polack and his grocery orders runs my poor little tail to a frazzle."

He crossed his arms over his chest and stretched out his legs, yawning beneath his baseball cap.

"The hell you say," said Wally. "Come on, you guys."

They all jumped on Muskrat, each grabbing a leg or an arm, and started carrying him over the lot toward 26th Street.

"Man, I'm telling you, this is a sin. This is one tired boy you're carrying off." He wriggled and tried to get free. "Rape! Rape!" he hollered.

They carried him for a couple of blocks, then set him on his feet. He slouched along behind them, his hands stuffed deep in his pockets and his cap pulled low over his eyes, grumbling to himself.

"Man, I gets fighty when I'm drinking."

"Yeah, yeah. We know all about it," said Wally.

"I sure hope it's a good picture," said Little Joe. "I sure hope it's got some beautiful women in it."

"Man, don't sit next to me if you're gonna start playing with yourself again," Muskrat said.

"Go to hell."

"You wait'll you get home this time," grumbled Muskrat. "Man, that's the trouble with us. All we got's Rosemary. I might just as well be back in Jamesburg as be here, irregardless of how much tail walks the street. I sure wisht I had three bucks. I sure wisht I did. I'd treat myself to something nice. I seen this little old brown girl in a pretty blue dress the other night. On Federal Street it was. And she had a flower in her hair and as she's coming up the street I can smell her perfume coming at me, and as she passes she says, without even looking my way, she says, 'Three bucks.' 'Three bucks,' she says, 'cause, you know, she ain't no charity whore like Rosemary. Then she goes pretends to look at the junk in the five-and-dime window, kinda waiting to see what I'd do, you know. But all I could do was stand and look at her, 'cause, man, I sure in hell didn't have no three bucks. So she waits and watches me outa the corner of her eye, and when she sees me hesitating, she sorta sniffs at me and kicks up her pumps and walks off. Made me madder'n hell. If I only had them three bucks."

"Whyn't you save up on what the old Polack pays you?" said Wally.

"He barely *pays* me more'n three bucks a week and between that and what I can lift from the ole lady's purse, it hardly stretches to keep my poor ole tail and soul together. And you know it's harder'n hell for me to save. I'm so generous, you know."

"To your own gut," said Wally. "Muskrat, if you want something bad enough you'll go through hell and high water to get it."

"Hmph! Hmph!" snorted Muskrat, tugging at the peak of his baseball cap. "Now just listen to Parson Wallace, fellas. Just give a listen."

A policeman stepped out of an alley, stretching out his arms and blocking their way.

"Where you boys going?"

"What's that to you?" said Wally.

"Don't get wise with me, kid, or I'll—" He patted the long nightstick hanging at his belt.

"We ain't done nothing," said Wally, thrusting his hands on his hips and staring the policeman in the eye.

"Man, we're just out for a little evening stroll," said Muskrat.

"Keep quiet," said Wally.

"I ast you where you was going." The policeman unsnapped the nightstick from his belt and held it clenched at his side.

"We're out walking," said Wally.

"Oh, out walking, huh? Where?"

"None of your goddamned business."

The policeman lifted the stick high, threatening to strike.

"Don't get funny, kid. So Christ help me, I'll split your skull wide open."

Wally spit a lunger into the gutter and wiped his mouth slowly with the back of his hand.

"It's awful late for you boys to be out. Looks kinda funny."

"Man, this ain't Russia, you know," said Muskrat.

"Don't get sassy with me, kid, I'm telling you. You know damned well there's a nine o'clock curfew. Any kid out later than nine gets stopped, see?"

"We ain't up to nothing either, see?" Wally said.

"Yeah? Where'd you get the booze? The smell of the whole pack of you is enough to knock me over. There's not a one of you of age."

"My old man treated us to a little wine," said Wally. "It's my birthday."

"That's an old hooch story. Tell me another. Tell me who your old man is."

"Why do you pester him that way on his birthday?" said Muskrat, stepping up close to the policeman. "We're all witnesses—It's his birthday, like he says, and his old man breaks out a bottle for once. So it's an event, but, man, that don't give you no reason for trying to lock us up."

"What's your name, shorty? You'd make a damned good lawyer."

"Look, Muskrat, I told you to keep outa this, didn't I?"

"So, big boy, you wanta be the mouthpiece, eh? Just tell me where you're headed, that's all. Maybe you're going up the 'Vic' movies, eh? Maybe you're the guys that raped that girl in the men's toilet the other night."

"I ain't never raped nobody," said Muskrat, gloomily.

"Or maybe you belong to the milkbottle gang. Or maybe you're the guys that started the fire in the high school cellar. Or turned the car over on Federal Street last Friday night. How do I know? I gotta check, see? Gotta find out your names and addresses and where you're going. 'Cause it's after nine o'clock, see?"

"Man, you mean you ain't caught all them criminals yet?" said Muskrat. "Some police force, I'll say. Why, it's dangerous to walk the streets with a police force slow as that."

"Yeah, mister, you got it all right," said Wally. "You're on the job for once. And right now we're gonna catch a bus to Trenton."

"Well, well. And whata you gonna do there?" said the policeman, fingering his nightstick. "See the governor maybe?"

"Naw, to hell with the governor. Things are kinda dull in Camden. Not much left to do. So we're gonna hop the bus and go up and rob and rape old lady Roebling, see? You want an in?"

"Comedian, eh?" The policeman whacked Wally across the face with his stick. "Funny guy."

"Man, you sonofabitchin cop, you can't do that!" Muskrat squatted low in a football position and charged into the policeman, hitting him just below the knees. The policeman let out a yell and fell over backwards, his nightstick flying out of his hand and clattering away over the pavement.

"Haul ass!" shouted Muskrat, spinning around and shooing his arms at the others. He grabbed hold of Wally. The boys turned on their heels and started to run up the dark street. Behind came the shrill whistle of the policeman.

"Don't stop till you get to the lot!" panted Wally, turning to glance back as they raced around a corner. "Ole cop's still flat on his back!"

"I shoulda cut his windpipe," said Muskrat. "Just listen to him toot." He glanced over at Wally, who was running beside Lipper.

"Did he hurt you?"

"Like to broke my nose," said Wally. "I'll be all right."

They crossed 26th Street and as they were running over the lot, Little Joe tripped and sprawled flat on his face. Wally caught Muskrat by the arm and pulled him back to where Little Joe had fallen. They took hold of him and dragged him over to the truck. Hector and Lipper were already inside. Lipper was holding open the canvas flap and jumping up and down with excitement.

"Hurry up, you guys, hurry up!" he called in a hoarse whisper.

Wally and Muskrat boosted Little Joe up into the truck and they piled in after.

"Watch out for the broken glass, you guys," said Wally.

"Man, damn that Greek. I feel it crunching under foot," said Muskrat, all out of breath. "I sure wish we had a light so I could see where I'm stepping."

"No lights, " said Wally.

They became silent, listening, all of them sweating and breathing hard from the run.

"You okay, Little Joe?" Wally said.

"I'm okay. Hell, I shoudn'ta tripped over my own feet like that. You guys mighta got caught."

"That cop's probably still flat on his ass," sneered Muskrat.

Wally went to the canvas flap, opened it cautiously and peered out.

"You know, that cop had shins like iron bars," said Muskrat. "I never come across a set o' bones like that in all my life. My shoulder's still aching."

"Don't talk so loud," whispered Wally.

"Why, man? What's you see?" said Muskrat, lowering his voice.

"There's a car coming slow down 26th Street."

"Hell, that ain't nothing. Plenty cars come down 26th Street."

"What'll we do?" said Little Joe.

"Yeah, what if it is the cops?" said Hector.

"We can't do nothing but sit here and keep quiet," said Wally. "Don't nobody light any cigarets or anything. I'm going to hold the flap open and keep a lookout."

"Man, I ain't *got* any cigarets to light," said Muskrat. "Hell, boys, ain't this just like a movie?"

"Don't talk so loud," said Wally.

"I only wisht you hadn't mentioned cigarets, that's all," whispered Muskrat. "Makes me hungry for one."

The truck grew quiet. Wally watched as the automobile cruised down 26th Street. It made a U-turn at the corner and came back again, a brilliant spotlight, hitched to the side of the car, moving slowly back and forth across the empty lot.

"It's them," said Wally. "They didn't waste much time."

"Manoman, and me still out on good behavior," said Muskrat. "Dear, sweet Jamesburg, here I come again," he sighed.

A sniffling noise came from somewhere in the darkness of the truck. The truck trembled a little, creaking lightly on the springs.

"Who's that?" said Wally.

"I wanta get outa here," said Lipper in a choking voice. "I don't wanta go to Jamesburg."

"Nobody's going to Jamesburg," said Wally. "Cut out that crying."

"I wanta get outa here," repeated Lipper, shaking the truck with his sobs.

"Man, stop that blubbering," whispered Muskrat. "If anybody goes to Jamesburg it'll be *me*. Who knocked that cop on his ass, anyway?"

"You did," cried Lipper. "I seen you do it, Muskrat."

"Well, just don't you squeal," said Muskrat. He reached out for Lipper, but Lipper crawled away into a corner, pressing himself up tight in it.

"Stop moving around, you guys," said Wally. "And quit the talking."

"Yeah, and who's got a record a mile long?" whispered Muskrat angrily. "You think you got something to cry about . . . Ah shit!" He laughed softly. "Hey, Wally, you know, this'll be my third time up? Back home for me, boys. I'll be seeing you all in a couple of years."

The car had turned around, the spotlight still playing over the lot. The car stopped and the light made a fast sweep over the flat ground in the direction of the truck, picked it out and rested there. A thin bar of light cut in through the chink in the canvas where Wally was looking out. It threw a faint illumination into the truck so that the boys could see each other's faces, pale and tense. Wally closed the chink and sank down on the floor.

"Goddamn it," he said.

"I wanta get outa here," said Lipper, and started to cry again.

"Are they coming?" said Hector.

"They got us spotted."

"You think maybe I shouldn'ta tackled that cop, Wally?"

"Hell, no!"

"I wanta get outa here," said Lipper.

"Goddamn you, Lipper . . ."

"Shutup," Wally said. He kneeled up and pulled open the flap a little. The same bar of light shot in through the chink. He looked out and saw the flashlights playing over the lot and moving in the direction of the truck. He pulled the flap to.

"They're coming," he said. "Just sit tight and act casual."

"You think that cop'll remember us?" whispered Hector.

"He'd have to be blind if he don't," said Wally.

"Let me outa here!" cried Lipper, leaping up and stumbling toward the rear of the truck.

"Get back here, you crazy sonuvabitch," said Wally. He grabbed Lipper around the knees and dragged him into his lap, keeping a tight hold on him.

"If you run out they'll shoot you."

"I don't wanta go to Jamesburg," sobbed Lipper, struggling to get free of Wally.

"Man, Jamesburg ain't so bad," said Muskrat. "You oughtn't to talk that way. I been there. I know—But, you know, I sure wish I could pull stunts like the one that cop told us happened up at the 'Vic's' craphouse. They don't seem to catch them guys."

"Listen!" said Hector.

From outside came the sound of footsteps moving closer to the truck. There were low voices, but the boys couldn't make out what was being said. They sat waiting, hardly moving, trying to catch the words.